For ♡ P9-CER-770
 off non-legal reading.
Happy Birthday!

5-14-84

love,
Lili + Rollin

NABOKOV'S DOZEN

NABOKOV'S DOZEN

A Collection of Thirteen Stories

by
Vladimir Nabokov

Anchor Press/Doubleday
Garden City, New York
1984

The stories "Conversation Piece," "First Love," "Signs and Symbols," and "Lance," appeared originally in *The New Yorker.*

Library of Congress Cataloging in Publication Data

Nabokov, Vladimir Vladimirovich, 1899–1977.
    Nabokov's dozen.

    I. Title.
PS3527.A15A6 1984b   813'.54   83-45237
ISBN 0-385-19117-0 (pbk.)

Library of Congress Cataloging in Publication Data to come:
ISBN 0-385-19117-0

CONTENTS

NABOKOV'S DOZEN

Spring in Fialta

Spring in Fialta is cloudy and dull. Everything is damp: the piebald trunks of the plane trees, the juniper shrubs, the railings, the gravel. Far away, in a watery vista between the jagged edges of pale bluish houses, which have tottered up from their knees to climb the slope (a cypress indicating the way), the blurred Mount St. George is more than ever remote from its likeness on the picture post cards which since 1910, say (those straw hats, those youthful cabmen), have been courting the tourist from the sorry-go-round of their prop, among amethyst-toothed lumps of rock and the mantelpiece dreams of sea shells. The air is windless and warm, with a faint tang of burning. The sea, its salt drowned in a solution of rain, is less glaucous than gray with waves too sluggish to break into foam.

It was on such a day in the early thirties that I found myself, all my senses wide open, on one of Fialta's steep little streets, taking in everything at once, that marine rococo on the stand, and the coral crucifixes in a shopwindow, and the dejected poster of a visiting circus, one corner of its drenched paper detached from the wall, and a yellow bit of unripe orange peel on the old, slate-blue sidewalk, which retained here and there a fading memory of ancient mosaic design. I am fond of Fialta; I am fond of it because I feel in the hollow of those violaceous syllables the sweet dark dampness of the most rumpled of small flowers, and because the altolike name of a lovely Crimean town is echoed by its viola; and also because there is something in the very somnolence of its humid Lent that especially anoints one's soul. So I was happy to be there again, to trudge uphill in inverse direction to the rivulet of the gutter, hatless, my head wet, my skin already suffused with warmth although I wore only a light mackintosh over my shirt.

I had come on the Capparabella express, which, with that reckless gusto peculiar to trains in mountainous country, had done its thundering best to collect throughout the night as many tunnels as possible. A day or two, just as long as a breathing spell in the midst of a business trip would allow me, was all I expected to stay. I had left my wife and children at home, and that was an island of happiness always present in the clear north of my being, always floating beside me, and even through me, I dare say, but yet keeping on the outside of me most of the time.

A pantless infant of the male sex, with a taut mud-gray little belly, jerkily stepped down from a doorstep and waddled off, bowlegged, trying to carry three oranges at once, but continuously dropping the variable third, until he fell himself, and then a girl of twelve or so, with a string of heavy beads around her dusky neck and wearing a skirt as long as that of a gypsy, promptly took away the whole lot with her more nimble and more numerous hands. Nearby, on the wet terrace of a café, a waiter was wiping the slabs of tables; a melancholy brigand hawking local lollipops, elaborate-looking things with a lunar gloss, had placed a hopelessly full basket on the cracked balustrade, over which the two were conversing. Either the drizzle had stopped or Fialta had got so used to it that she herself did not know whether she was breathing moist air or warm rain. Thumb-filling his pipe from a rubber pouch as he walked, a plus-foured Englishman of the solid exportable sort came from under an arch and entered a pharmacy, where large pale sponges in a blue vase were dying a thirsty death behind their glass. What luscious elation I felt rippling through my veins, how gratefully my whole being responded to the flutters and effluvia of that gray day saturated with a vernal essence which itself it seemed slow in perceiving! My nerves were unusually receptive after a sleepless night; I assimilated everything: the whistling of a thrush in the almond trees beyond the chapel, the peace of the crumbling houses, the pulse of the distant sea, panting in the mist, all this together with the jealous green of bottle glass bristling along the top of a wall and the fast colors of a circus advertisement featuring a feathered Indian on a rearing horse in the act of lassoing a boldly endemic zebra, while some thoroughly fooled elephants sat brooding upon their star-spangled thrones.

Presently the same Englishman overtook me. As I absorbed him along with the rest, I happened to notice the sudden side-roll of his big blue eye straining at its crimson canthus, and the way he rapidly moistened his lips—because of the dryness of those sponges, I thought; but then I followed the direction of his glance, and saw Nina.

Every time I had met her during the fifteen years of our—
well, I fail to find the precise term for our kind of relationship—she had not seemed to recognize me at once; and this
time too she remained quite still for a moment, on the
opposite sidewalk, half turning toward me in sympathetic
incertitude mixed with curiosity, only her yellow scarf already on the move like those dogs that recognize you
before their owners do—and then she uttered a cry, her
hands up, all her ten fingers dancing, and in the middle of
the street, with merely the frank impulsiveness of an old
friendship (just as she would rapidly make the sign of the
cross over me every time we parted), she kissed me thrice
with more mouth than meaning, and then walked beside
me, hanging on to me, adjusting her stride to mine, hampered by her narrow brown skirt perfunctorily slit down
the side.

"Oh yes, Ferdie is here too," she replied and immediately
in her turn inquired nicely after Elena.

"Must be loafing somewhere around with Segur," she
went on in reference to her husband. "And I have some
shopping to do; we leave after lunch. Wait a moment, where
are you leading me, Victor dear?"

Back into the past, back into the past, as I did every time
I met her, repeating the whole accumulation of the plot
from the very beginning up to the last increment—thus in
Russian fairy tales the already told is bunched up again
at every new turn of the story. This time we had met in
warm and misty Fialta, and I could not have celebrated the
occasion with greater art, could not have adorned with
brighter vignettes the list of fate's former services, even if
I had known that this was to be the last one; the last one,
I maintain, for I cannot imagine any heavenly firm of

brokers that might consent to arrange me a meeting with her beyond the grave.

My introductory scene with Nina had been laid in Russia quite a long time ago, around 1917 I should say, judging by certain left-wing theater rumblings backstage. It was at some birthday party at my aunt's on her country estate, near Luga, in the deepest folds of winter (how well I remember the first sign of nearing the place: a red barn in a white wilderness). I had just graduated from the Imperial Lyceum; Nina was already engaged: although she was of my age and of that of the century, she looked twenty at least, and this in spite or perhaps because of her neat slender build, whereas at thirty-two that very slightness of hers made her look younger. Her fiancé was a guardsman on leave from the front, a handsome heavy fellow, incredibly well-bred and stolid, who weighed every word on the scales of the most exact common sense and spoke in a velvety baritone, which grew even smoother when he addressed her; his decency and devotion probably got on her nerves; and he is now a successful if somewhat lonesome engineer in a most distant tropical country.

Windows light up and stretch their luminous lengths upon the dark billowy snow, making room for the reflection of the fan-shaped light above the front door between them. Each of the two side-pillars is fluffily fringed with white, which rather spoils the lines of what might have been a perfect ex libris for the book of our two lives. I cannot recall why we had all wandered out of the sonorous hall into the still darkness, peopled only with firs, snow-swollen to twice their size; did the watchmen invite us to look at a sullen red glow in the sky, portent of nearing arson? Possibly. Did we go to admire an equestrian statue of ice sculptured near the pond by the Swiss tutor of my cousins? Quite as likely.

My memory revives only on the way back to the brightly symmetrical mansion towards which we tramped in single file along a narrow furrow between snowbanks, with that crunch-crunch-crunch which is the only comment that a taciturn winter night makes upon humans. I walked last; three singing steps ahead of me walked a small bent shape; the firs gravely showed their burdened paws. I slipped and dropped the dead flashlight someone had forced upon me; it was devilishly hard to retrieve; and instantly attracted by my curses, with an eager, low laugh in anticipation of fun, Nina dimly veered toward me. I call her Nina, but I could hardly have known her name yet, hardly could we have had time, she and I, for any preliminary; "Who's that?" she asked with interest—and I was already kissing her neck, smooth and quite fiery hot from the long fox fur of her coat collar, which kept getting into my way until she clasped my shoulder, and with the candor so peculiar to her gently fitted her generous, dutiful lips to mine.

But suddenly parting us by its explosion of gaiety, the theme of a snowball fight started in the dark, and someone, fleeing, falling, crunching, laughing and panting, climbed a drift, tried to run, and uttered a horrible groan: deep snow had performed the amputation of an arctic. And soon after, we all dispersed to our respective homes, without my having talked with Nina, nor made any plans about the future, about those fifteen itinerant years that had already set out toward the dim horizon, loaded with the parts of our unassembled meetings; and as I watched her in the maze of gestures and shadows of gestures of which the rest of that evening consisted (probably parlor games—with Nina persistently in the other camp), I was astonished, I remember, not so much by her inattention to me after that warmth in the snow as by the innocent naturalness of that inattention, for I did not yet know that had I said a word it would have changed at once into a wonderful sunburst of kindness, a cheerful, compassionate attitude with all possible co-operation, as if woman's love were spring water containing salubrious salts which at the least notice she ever so willingly gave anyone to drink.

"Let me see, where did we last meet," I began (addressing the Fialta version of Nina) in order to bring to her small face with prominent cheekbones and dark-red lips a certain expression I knew; and sure enough, the shake of her head and the puckered brow seemed less to imply forgetfulness than to deplore the flatness of an old joke; or to be more exact, it was as if all those cities where fate had fixed our various rendezvous without ever attending them personally, all those platforms and stairs and three-walled rooms and dark back alleys, were trite settings remaining after some other lives all brought to a close long before and were so little related to the acting out of our own aimless destiny that it was almost bad taste to mention them.

I accompanied her into a shop under the arcades; there, in the twilight beyond a beaded curtain, she fingered some red leather purses stuffed with tissue paper, peering at the price tags, as if wishing to learn their museum names. She wanted, she said, exactly that shape but in fawn, and when after ten minutes of frantic rustling the old Dalmatian found such a freak by a miracle that has puzzled me ever since, Nina, who was about to pick some money out of my hand, changed her mind and went through the streaming beads without having bought anything.

Outside it was just as milky dull as before; the same smell of burning, stirring my Tartar memories, drifted from the bare windows of the pale houses; a small swarm of gnats was busy darning the air above a mimosa, which bloomed

listlessly, her sleeves trailing to the very ground; two work-
men in broad-brimmed hats were lunching on cheese and
garlic, their backs against a circus billboard, which depicted
a red hussar and an orange tiger of sorts; curious—in his
effort to make the beast as ferocious as possible, the artist
had gone so far that he had come back from the other side,
for the tiger's face looked positively human.

"*Au fond*, I wanted a comb," said Nina with belated regret.

How familiar to me were her hesitations, second
thoughts, third thoughts mirroring first ones, ephemeral
worries between trains. She had always either just arrived
or was about to leave, and of this I find it hard to think without feeling humiliated by the variety of intricate routes
one feverishly follows in order to keep that final appointment which the most confirmed dawdler knows to be un-
avoidable. Had I to submit before judges of our earthly
existence a specimen of her average pose, I would have
perhaps placed her leaning upon a counter at Cook's, left
calf crossing right shin, left toe tapping floor, sharp elbows
and coin-spilling bag on the counter, while the employee,
pencil in hand, pondered with her over the plan of an
eternal sleeping car.

After the exodus from Russia, I saw her—and that was the
second time—in Berlin at the house of some friends. I was
about to get married; she had just broken with her fiancé.
As I entered that room I caught sight of her at once and,
having glanced at the other guests, I instinctively determined which of the men knew more about her than I. She
was sitting in the corner of a couch, her feet pulled up, her
small comfortable body folded in the form of a Z; an ash
tray stood aslant on the couch near one of her heels; and,
having squinted at me and listened to my name, she re-

moved her stalklike cigarette holder from her lips and proceeded to utter slowly and joyfully, "Well, of all people—"
and at once it became clear to everyone, beginning with her,
that we had long been on intimate terms: unquestionably,
she had forgotten all about the actual kiss, but somehow
because of that trivial occurrence she found herself recol-
lecting a vague stretch of warm, pleasant friendship, which
in reality had never existed between us. Thus the whole cast
of our relationship was fraudulently based upon an imaginary amity—which had nothing to do with her random good
will. Our meeting proved quite insignificant in regard to
the words we said, but already no barriers divided us;
and when that night I happened to be seated beside her
at supper, I shamelessly tested the extent of her secret
patience.

Then she vanished again; and a year later my wife and I
were seeing my brother off to Posen, and when the train had
gone, and we were moving toward the exit along the other
side of the platform, suddenly near a car of the Paris express I saw Nina, her face buried in the bouquet she held, in
the midst of a group of people whom she had befriended
without my knowledge and who stood in a circle gaping at
her as idlers gape at a street row, a lost child, or the victim
of an accident. Brightly she signaled to me with her flowers;
I introduced her to Elena, and in that life-quickening atmosphere of a big railway station where everything is something trembling on the brink of something else, thus to be
clutched and cherished, the exchange of a few words was
enough to enable two totally dissimilar women to start
calling each other by their pet names the very next time
they met. That day, in the blue shade of the Paris car,
Ferdinand was first mentioned: I learned with a ridiculous
pang that she was about to marry him. Doors were begin-

ning to slam; she quickly but piously kissed her friends, climbed into the vestibule, disappeared; and then I saw her through the glass settling herself in her compartment, having suddenly forgotten about us or passed into another world, and we all, our hands in our pockets, seemed to be spying upon an utterly unsuspecting life moving in that aquarium dimness, until she grew aware of us and drummed on the windowpane, then raised her eyes, fumbling at the frame as if hanging a picture, but nothing happened; some fellow passenger helped her, and she leaned out, audible and real, beaming with pleasure; one of us, keeping up with the stealthily gliding car, handed her a magazine and a Tauchnitz (she read English only when traveling); all was slipping away with beautiful smoothness, and I held a platform ticket crumpled beyond recognition, while a song of the last century (connected, it has been rumored, with some Parisian drama of love) kept ringing and ringing in my head, having emerged, God knows why, from the music box of memory, a sobbing ballad which often used to be sung by an old maiden aunt of mine, with a face as yellow as Russian church wax, but whom nature had given such a powerful, ecstatically full voice that it seemed to swallow her up in the glory of a fiery cloud as soon as she would begin:

On dit que tu te maries,
tu sais que j'en vais mourir,

and that melody, the pain, the offense, the link between hymen and death evoked by the ryhthm, and the voice itself of the dead singer, which accompanied the recollection as the sole owner of the song, gave me no rest for several hours after Nina's departure and even later arose at increasing intervals like the last flat little waves sent to the beach by a passing ship, lapping ever more infrequently and dreamily, or like the bronze agony of a vibrating belfry after the bell ringer has already reseated himself in the cheerful circle of his family. And another year or two later, I was in Paris on business; and one morning on the landing of a hotel, where I had been looking up a film-actor fellow, there she was again, clad in a gray tailored suit, waiting for the elevator to take her down, a key dangling from her fingers. "Ferdinand has gone fencing," she said conversationally; her eyes rested on the lower part of my face as if she were lip reading, and after a moment of reflection (her amatory comprehension was matchless), she turned and rapidly swaying on slender ankles led me along the sea-blue carpeted passage. A chair at the door of her room supported a tray with the remains of breakfast—a honeystained knife, crumbs on the gray porcelain; but the room had already been done, and because of our sudden draft a wave of muslin embroidered with white dahlias got sucked in, with a shudder and knock, between the responsive halves of the French window, and only when the door had been locked did they let go that curtain with something like a blissful sigh; and a little later I stepped out on the diminutive cast-iron balcony beyond to inhale a combined smell of dry maple leaves and gasoline—the dregs of the hazy blue morning street; and as I did not yet realize the presence of that growing morbid pathos which was to embitter so my subsequent meetings with Nina, I was probably quite as collected and carefree as she was, when from the hotel I accompanied her to some office or other to trace a suitcase she had lost, and thence to the café where her husband was holding session with his court of the moment.

I will not mention the name (and what bits of it I happen

to give here appear in decorous disguise) of that man, that Franco-Hungarian writer. . . . I would rather not dwell upon him at all, but I cannot help it—he is surging up from under my pen. Today one does not hear much about him; and this is good, for it proves that I was right in resisting his evil spell, right in experiencing a creepy chill down my spine whenever this or that new book of his touched my hand. The fame of his likes circulates briskly but soon grows heavy and stale; and as for history it will limit his life story to the dash between two dates. Lean and arrogant, with some poisonous pun ever ready to fork out and quiver at you, and with a strange look of expectancy in his dull brown veiled eyes, this false wag had, I daresay, an irresistible effect on small rodents. Having mastered the art of verbal invention to perfection, he particularly prided himself on being a weaver of words, a title he valued higher than that of a writer; personally, I never could understand what was the good of thinking up books, of penning things that had not really happened in some way or other; and I remember once saying to him as I braved the mockery of his encouraging nods that, were I a writer, I should allow only my heart to have imagination, and for the rest rely upon memory, that long-drawn sunset shadow of one's personal truth.

I had known his books before I knew him; a faint disgust was already replacing the aesthetic pleasure which I had suffered his first novel to give me. At the beginning of his career, it had been possible perhaps to distinguish some human landscape, some old garden, some dream-familiar disposition of trees through the stained glass of his prodigious prose . . . but with every new book the tints grew still more dense, the gules and purpure still more ominous; and today one can no longer see anything at all through that blazoned, ghastly rich glass, and it seems that were one to break it, nothing but a perfectly black void would face one's shivering soul. But how dangerous he was in his prime, what venom he squirted, with what whips he lashed when provoked! The tornado of his passing satire left a barren waste where felled oaks lay in a row, and the dust still twisted, and the unfortunate author of some adverse review, howling with pain, spun like a top in the dust.

At the time we met, his *"Passage à niveau"* was being acclaimed in Paris; he was, as they say, "surrounded," and Nina (whose adaptability was an amazing substitute for the culture she lacked) had already assumed if not the part of a muse at least that of a soul mate and subtle adviser, following Ferdinand's creative convolutions and loyally sharing his artistic tastes; for although it is wildly improbable that she had ever waded through a single volume of his, she had a magic knack of gleaning all the best passages from the shop talk of literary friends.

An orchestra of women was playing when we entered the café; first I noted the ostrich thigh of a harp reflected in one of the mirror-faced pillars, and then I saw the composite table (small ones drawn together to form a long one) at which, with his back to the plush wall, Ferdinand was presiding; and for a moment his whole attitude, the position of his parted hands, and the faces of his table companions all turned toward him reminded me in a grotesque, nightmarish way of something I did not quite grasp, but when I did so in retrospect, the suggested comparison struck me as hardly less sacrilegious than the nature of his art itself. He wore a white turtle-neck sweater under a tweed coat; his glossy hair was combed back from the temples, and above it cigarette smoke hung like a halo; his bony, Pharaohlike face was motionless: the eyes alone roved this way and that, full of dim satisfaction. Having forsaken the two or three obvious haunts where naïve amateurs of Montparnassian life would have expected to find him, he had started patronizing this perfectly bourgeois establishment because of his peculiar sense of humor, which made him derive ghoulish fun from the pitiful *specialité de la maison* —this orchestra composed of half a dozen weary-looking, self-conscious ladies interlacing mild harmonies on a crammed platform and not knowing, as he put it, what to do with their motherly bosoms, quite superfluous in the world of music. After each number he would be convulsed by a fit of epileptic applause, which the ladies had stopped acknowledging and which was already arousing, I thought, certain doubts in the minds of the proprietor of the café and its fundamental customers, but which seemed highly diverting to Ferdinand's friends. Among these I recall: an artist with an impeccably bald though slightly chipped head, which under various pretexts he constantly painted into his eye-and-guitar canvases; a poet, whose special gag was the ability to represent, if you asked him, Adam's Fall by means of five matches; a humble business man who financed surrealist ventures (and paid for the *apéritifs*) if permitted to print in a corner eulogistic allusions to the actress he kept; a pianist, presentable insofar as the face was concerned, but with a dreadful expression of the fingers; a jaunty but linguistically impotent Soviet writer fresh from Moscow, with an old pipe and a new wrist watch, who was completely and ridiculously unaware of the sort of company he was in; there were several other gentlemen present who have become confused in my memory, and doubtless two or three of the lot had been intimate with Nina. She was the only woman at the table; there she stooped, eagerly sucking at a straw, the level of her lemonade sinking with a kind of childish celerity, and only when the last drop had gurgled and squeaked, and she had pushed away the straw with her tongue, only then did I finally catch her eye, which I had been obstinately seeking, still not being able to cope with the fact that she had had time to forget what had occurred earlier in the morning—to forget it so thoroughly that upon meeting my glance, she replied with a blank questioning smile, and only after peering more closely did she remember suddenly what kind of answering smile I was expecting. Meanwhile, Ferdinand (the ladies having temporarily left the platform after pushing away their instruments like so many pieces of furniture) was juicily drawing his cronies' attention to the figure of an elderly luncher in a far corner of the café, who had, as some Frenchmen for some reason or other have, a little red ribbon or something on his coat lapel and whose gray beard combined with his mustaches to form a cosy yellowish nest for his sloppily munching mouth. Somehow the trappings of old age always amused Ferdie.

I did not stay long in Paris, but that week proved sufficient to engender between him and me that fake chumminess the imposing of which he had such a talent for. Subsequently I even turned out to be of some use to him: my firm acquired the film rights of one of his more intelligible stories, and then he had a good time pestering me with telegrams. As the years passed, we found ourselves every now and then beaming at each other in some place, but I never felt at ease in his presence, and that day in Fialta, too, I experienced a familiar depression upon learning that he was on the prowl nearby; one thing, however, considerably cheered me up: the flop of his recent play.

And here he was coming toward us, garbed in an absolutely waterproof coat with belt and pocket flaps, a camera across his shoulder, double rubber soles to his shoes, sucking with an imperturbability that was meant to be funny a long stick of moonstone candy, that specialty of Fialta's. Beside him, walked the dapper, doll-like, rosy Segur, a lover of art and a perfect fool; I never could discover for what purpose Ferdinand needed him; and I still hear Nina exclaiming with a moaning tenderness that did not commit her to anything: "Oh, he is such a darling, Segur!" They approached; Ferdinand and I greeted each other lustily, trying to crowd into hand shake and back slap as much fervor as possible, knowing by experience that actually that was all but pretending it was only a preface; and it always happened like that: after every separation we met to the accompaniment of strings being excitedly tuned, in a bustle of geniality, in the hubbub of sentiments taking their seats; but the ushers would close the doors, and after that no one was admitted.

Segur complained to me about the weather, and at first I did not understand what he was talking about; even if the moist, gray, greenhouse essence of Fialta might be called "weather," it was just as much outside of anything that could serve us as a topic of conversation as was, for instance, Nina's slender elbow, which I was holding between finger and thumb, or a bit of tin foil someone had dropped, shining in the middle of the cobbled street in the distance.

We four moved on, vague purchases still looming ahead. "God, what an Indian!" Ferdinand suddenly exclaimed with fierce relish, violently nudging me and pointing at a poster. Further on, near a fountain, he gave his stick of candy to a native child, a swarthy girl with beads round her pretty neck; we stopped to wait for him: he crouched saying something to her, addressing her sooty-black lowered eyelashes, and then he caught up with us, grinning and making one of those remarks with which he loved to spice his speech. Then his attention was drawn by an unfortunate object exhibited in a souvenir shop: a dreadful marble imitation of Mount St. George showing a black tunnel at its base, which turned out to be the mouth of an inkwell, and with a compartment for pens in the semblance of railroad tracks. Open-mouthed, quivering, all agog with sardonic triumph, he turned that dusty, cumbersome, and perfectly irresponsible thing in his hands, paid without bargaining, and with his mouth still open came out carrying the monster. Like some autocrat who surrounds himself with hunchbacks and dwarfs, he would become attached to this or that hideous object; this infatuation might last from five minutes to several days or even longer if the thing happened to be animate.

Nina wistfully alluded to lunch, and seizing the opportunity when Ferdinand and Segur stopped at a post office, I hastened to lead her away. I still wonder what exactly she meant to me, that small dark woman of the narrow shoulders and "lyrical limbs" (to quote the expression of a mincing émigré poet, one of the few men who had sighed platonically after her), and still less do I understand what was the purpose of fate in bringing us constantly together. I did not see her for quite a long while after my sojourn in Paris, and then one day when I came home from my office I found her having tea with my wife and examining on her silk-hosed hand, with her wedding ring gleaming through, the texture of some stockings bought cheap in Tauentzien-strasse. Once I was shown her photograph in a fashion magazine full of autumn leaves and gloves and wind-swept golf links. On a certain Christmas she sent me a picture post card with snow and stars. On a Riviera beach she almost escaped my notice behind her dark glasses and terra-cotta tan. Another day, having dropped in on an ill-timed errand at the house of some strangers where a party was in progress, I saw her scarf and fur coat among alien scarecrows on a coat rack. In a bookshop she nodded to me from a page of one of her husband's stories, a page referring to an episodic servant girl, but smuggling in Nina in spite of the author's intention: "Her face," he wrote, "was rather nature's snapshot than a meticulous portrait, so that when . . . tried to imagine it, all he could visualize were fleeting glimpses of disconnected features: the downy outline of her pommettes in the sun, the amber-tinted brown darkness of quick eyes, lips shaped into a friendly smile which was always ready to change into an ardent kiss."

Again and again she hurriedly appeared in the margins of my life, without influencing in the least its basic text. One summer morning (Friday—because housemaids were thumping out carpets in the sun-dusted yard), my family was away in the country and I was lolling and smoking in bed when I heard the bell ring with tremendous violence— and there she was in the hall having burst in to leave (incidentally) a hairpin and (mainly) a trunk illuminated with hotel labels, which a fortnight later was retrieved for her by a nice Austrian boy, who (according to intangible but sure symptoms) belonged to the same very cosmopolitan association of which I was a member. Occasionally, in the middle of a conversation her name would be mentioned, and she would run down the steps of a chance sentence, without turning her head. While traveling in the Pyrenees, I spent a week at the château belonging to people with whom she and Ferdinand happened to be staying, and I shall never forget my first night there: how I waited, how certain I was that without my having to tell her she would steal to my room, how she did not come, and the din thousands of crickets made in the delirious depth of the rocky garden dripping with moonlight, the mad bubbling brooks, and my struggle between blissful southern fatigue after a long day of hunting on the screes and the wild thirst for her stealthy coming, low laugh, pink ankles above the swan's-down trimming of high-heeled slippers; but the night raved on, and she did not come, and when next day, in the course of a general ramble in the mountains, I told her of my wait-ing, she clasped her hands in dismay—and at once with a rapid glance estimated whether the backs of the gesticulat-ing Ferd and his friend had sufficiently receded. I remem-ber talking to her on the telephone across half of Europe (on her husband's business) and not recognizing at first her eager barking voice; and I remember once dreaming of her: I dreamt that my eldest girl had run in to tell me the door-man was sorely in trouble—and when I had gone down to him, I saw lying on a trunk, a roll of burlap under her head, pale-lipped and wrapped in a woolen kerchief, Nina fast asleep, as miserable refugees sleep in Godforsaken railway stations. And regardless of what happened to me or to her, in between, we never discussed anything, as we never thought of each other during the intervals in our destiny, so that when we met the pace of life altered at once, all its atoms were recombined, and we lived in another, lighter time-medium, which was measured not by the lengthy separations but by those few meetings of which a short, supposedly frivolous life was thus artificially formed. And with each new meeting I grew more and more appre-hensive; no—I did not experience any inner emotional col-lapse, the shadow of tragedy did not haunt our revels, my married life remained unimpaired, while on the other hand her eclectic husband ignored her casual affairs although deriving some profit from them in the way of pleasant and useful connections. I grew apprehensive because something lovely, delicate, and unrepeatable was being wasted: something which I abused by snapping off poor bright bits in gross haste while neglecting the modest but true core which perhaps it kept offering me in a pitiful whisper. I was apprehensive because, in the long run, I was somehow accepting Nina's life, the lies, the futility, the gibberish of that life. Even in the absence of any sentimental discord, I felt myself bound to seek for a rational, if not moral, interpretation of my existence, and this meant choosing between the world in which I sat for my portrait, with my wife, my young daughters, the Doberman pinscher (idyllic garlands, a signet ring, a slender cane), between that happy, wise, and good world . . . and what? Was there any practical chance of life together with Nina, life I could barely imagine, for it would be penetrated, I knew, with a passionate, intolerable bitterness and every moment of it would be aware of a past, teeming with protean partners. No, the thing was absurd. And moreover was she not chained to her husband by something stronger than love—the stanch friendship between two convicts? Absurd! But then what should I have done with you, Nina, how should I have disposed of the store of sadness that had gradually accumulated as a result of our seemingly carefree, but really hopeless meetings?

Fialta consists of the old town and of the new one; here and there, past and present are interlaced, struggling either to disentangle themselves or to thrust each other out; each one has its own methods: the newcomer fights honestly—importing palm trees, setting up smart tourist agencies, painting with creamy lines the red smoothness of tennis courts; whereas the sneaky old-timer creeps out from behind a corner in the shape of some little street on crutches or the steps of stairs leading nowhere. On our way to the hotel, we passed a half-built white villa, full of litter within, on a wall of which again the same elephants, their monstrous baby knees wide apart, sat on huge, gaudy drums; in ethereal bundles the equestrienne (already with a penciled mustache) was resting on a broad-backed steed; and a tomato-nosed clown was walking a tightrope, balancing an umbrella ornamented with those recurrent stars— a vague symbolic recollection of the heavenly fatherland of circus performers. Here, in the Riviera part of Fialta, the wet gravel crunched in a more luxurious manner, and the lazy sighing of the sea was more audible. In the back yard of the hotel, a kitchen boy armed with a knife was pursuing a hen which was clucking madly as it raced for its life. A bootblack offered me his ancient throne with a toothless smile. Under the plane trees stood a motorcycle of German make, a mud-bespattered limousine, and a yellow longbodied Icarus that looked like a giant scarab: ("That's ours —Segur's, I mean," said Nina, adding, "Why don't you come with us, Victor?" although she knew very well that I could not come); in the lacquer of its elytra a gouache of sky and branches was engulfed; in the metal of one of the bomb-shaped lamps we ourselves were momentarily reflected, lean filmland pedestrians passing along the convex surface; and then, after a few steps, I glanced back and foresaw, in an almost optical sense, as it were, what really happened an hour or so later: the three of them wearing motoring helmets, getting in, smiling and waving to me, transparent to me like ghosts, with the color of the world shining through them, and then they were moving, receding, diminishing (Nina's last ten-fingered farewell); but actually the automobile was still standing quite motionless, smooth and whole like an egg, and Nina under my outstretched arm was entering a laurel-flanked doorway, and as we sat down we could see through the window Ferdinand and Segur, who had come by another way, slowly approaching.

There was no one on the veranda where we lunched except the Englishman I had recently observed; in front of him, a long glass containing a bright crimson drink threw an oval reflection on the tablecloth. In his eyes, I noticed the same bloodshot desire, but now it was in no sense related to Nina; that avid look was not directed at her at all, but was fixed on the upper right-hand corner of the broad window near which he was sitting.

Having pulled the gloves off her small thin hands, Nina, for the last time in her life, was eating the shellfish of which she was so fond. Ferdinand also busied himself with food, and I took advantage of his hunger to begin a conversation which gave me the semblance of power over him: to be specific, I mentioned his recent failure. After a brief period of fashionable religious conversion, during which grace descended upon him and he undertook some rather ambiguous pilgrimages, which ended in a decidedly scandalous adventure, he had turned his dull eyes toward barbarous Moscow. Now, frankly speaking, I have always been irritated by the complacent conviction that a ripple of stream consciousness, a few healthy obscenities, and a dash of communism in any old slop pail will alchemically and automatically produce ultramodern literature; and I will contend until I am shot that art as soon as it is brought into contact with politics inevitably sinks to the level of any ideological trash. In Ferdinand's case, it is true, all this was rather irrelevant: the muscles of his muse were exceptionally strong, to say nothing of the fact that he didn't care a damn for the plight of the underdog; but because of certain obscurely mischievous undercurrents of that sort, his art had become still more repulsive. Except for a few snobs none had understood the play; I had not seen it myself, but could well imagine that elaborate Kremlinesque night along the impossible spirals of which he spun various wheels of dismembered symbols; and now, not without pleasure, I asked him whether he had read a recent bit of criticism about himself.

"Criticism!" he exclaimed, "Fine criticism! Every slick jackanapes sees fit to read me a lecture. Ignorance of my work is their bliss. My books are touched gingerly, as one touches something that may go bang. Criticism! They are examined from every point of view except the essential one. It is as if a naturalist, in describing the equine genus, started to jaw about saddles or Mme. de V. (he named a well-known literary hostess, who indeed strongly resembled a grinning horse). I would like some of that pigeon's blood, too," he continued in the same loud, ripping voice, addressing the waiter, who understood his desire only after he had looked in the direction of the long-nailed finger which unceremoniously pointed at the Englishman's glass. For some reason or other, Segur mentioned Ruby Rose, the lady who painted flowers on her breast, and the conversation took on a less insulting character. Meanwhile the big Englishman suddenly made up his mind, got up on a chair, stepped from there on to the window sill, and stretched up till he reached that coveted corner of the frame where rested a compact furry moth, which he deftly slipped into a pillbox.

". . . rather like Wouwerman's white horse," said Ferdinand, in regard to something he was discussing with Segur.

"Tu es très hippique ce matin," remarked the latter.

Soon they both left to telephone. Ferdinand was particularly fond of long-distance calls, and particularly good at endowing them, no matter what the distance, with a friendly warmth when it was necessary, as for instance now, to make sure of free lodgings.

From afar came the sounds of music—a trumpet, a zither. Nina and I set out to wander again. The circus on its way to Fialta had apparently sent out runners: an advertising pageant was tramping by; but we did not catch its head, as it had turned uphill into a side alley: the gilded back of some carriage was receding, a man in a burnoose led a camel, a file of four mediocre Indians carried placards on poles, and behind them, by special permission, a tourist's small son in a sailor suit sat reverently on a tiny pony.

We wandered by a café where the tables were now almost dry but still empty; the waiter was examining (I hope he adopted it later) a horrible foundling, the absurd inkstand affair, stowed by Ferdinand on the banisters in passing. At the next corner we were attracted by an old stone stairway, and we climbed up, and I kept looking at the sharp angle of Nina's step as she ascended, raising her skirt, its narrowness requiring the same gesture as formerly length had done; she diffused a familiar warmth, and going up beside her, I recalled the last time we had come together. It had been in a Paris house, with many people around, and my dear friend Jules Darboux, wishing to do me a refined aesthetic favor, had touched my sleeve and said, "I want you to meet—" and led me to Nina, who sat in the corner of a couch, her body folded Z-wise, with an ash tray at her heel, and she took a long turquoise cigarette holder from her lips and joyfully, slowly exclaimed, "Well, of all people—" and then all evening my heart felt like breaking, as I passed from group to group with a sticky glass in my fist, now and then looking at her from a distance (she did not look . . .), and listened to scraps of conversation, and overheard one man saying to another, "Funny, how they all smell alike, burnt leaf through whatever perfume they use, those angular dark-haired girls," and as it often happens, a trivial remark related to some unknown topic coiled and clung to one's own intimate recollection, a parasite of its sadness.

At the top of the steps, we found ourselves on a rough kind of terrace. From here one could see the delicate outline of the dove-colored Mount St. George with a cluster of bone-white flecks (some hamlet) on one of its slopes; the smoke of an indiscernible train undulated along its rounded base—and suddenly disappeared; still lower, above the jumble of roofs, one could perceive a solitary cypress, resembling the moist-twirled black tip of a water-color brush; to the right, one caught a glimpse of the sea, which was gray, with silver wrinkles. At our feet lay a rusty old key, and on the wall of the half-ruined house adjoining the terrace, the ends of some wire still remained hanging . . . I reflected that formerly there had been life here, a family had enjoyed the coolness at nightfall, clumsy children had colored pictures by the light of a lamp . . . We lingered there as if listening to something; Nina, who stood on higher ground, put a hand on my shoulder and smiled, and carefully, so as not to crumple her smile, kissed me. With an unbearable force, I relived (or so it now seems to me) all that had ever been between us beginning with a similar kiss; and I said (substituting for our cheap, formal "thou" that strangely full and expressive "you" to which the circumnavigator, enriched all around, returns), "Look here—what if I love you?" Nina glanced at me, I repeated those words, I wanted to add . . . but something like a bat passed swiftly across her face, a quick, queer, almost ugly expression, and she, who would utter coarse words with perfect simplicity, became embarrassed; I also felt awkward . . . "Never mind, I was only joking," I hastened to say, lightly encircling her waist. From somewhere a firm bouquet of small dark, unselfishly smelling violets appeared in her hands, and before she returned to her husband and car, we stood for a little while longer by the stone parapet, and our romance was even more hopeless than it had ever been. But the stone was as warm as flesh, and suddenly I understood something I had been seeing without understanding— why a piece of tin foil had sparkled so on the pavement, why the gleam of a glass had trembled on a tablecloth, why the sea was ashimmer: somehow, by imperceptible degrees, the white sky above Fialta had got saturated with sunshine, and now it was sun-pervaded throughout, and this brimming white radiance grew broader and broader, all dissolved in it, all vanished, all passed, and I stood on the station platform of Mlech with a freshly bought newspaper, which told me that the yellow car I had seen under the plane trees had suffered a crash beyond Fialta, having run at full speed into the truck of a traveling circus entering the town, a crash from which Ferdinand and his friend, those invulnerable rogues, those salamanders of fate, those basilisks of good fortune, had escaped with local and temporary injury to their scales, while Nina, in spite of her long-standing, faithful imitation of them, had turned out after all to be mortal.

Paris, 1938.

A Forgotten Poet

1

In 1899, in the ponderous, comfortable padded St. Petersburg of those days, a prominent cultural organization, the Society for the Advancement of Russian Literature, decided to honor in a grand way the memory of the poet Konstantin Perov, who had died half a century before at the ardent age of four-and-twenty. He had been styled the Russian Rimbaud and, although the French boy surpassed him in genius, such a comparison is not wholly unjustified. When only eighteen he composed his remarkable *Georgian Nights,* a long, rambling "dream epic," certain passages of which rip the veil of its traditional Oriental setting to produce that heavenly draft which suddenly locates the sensorial effect of true poetry right between one's shoulder blades.

This was followed three years later by a volume of poems: he had got hold of some German philosopher or other, and several of these pieces are distressing because of the grotesque attempt at combining an authentic lyrical spasm with a metaphysical explanation of the universe; but the rest are still as vivid and unusual as they were in the days when that queer youth dislocated the Russian vocabulary and twisted the necks of accepted epithets in order to make poetry splutter and scream instead of twittering. Most readers like best those poems of his where the ideas of emancipation, so characteristic of the Russian fifties, are expressed in a glorious storm of obscure eloquence, which, as one critic put it, "does not show you the enemy but makes you fairly burst with the longing to fight." Personally I prefer the purer and at the same time bumpier lyrics such as "The Gypsy" or "The Bat."

Perov was the son of a small landowner of whom the only thing known is that he tried planting tea on his estate near Luga. Young Konstantin (to use a biographical intonation) spent most of his time in St. Petersburg vaguely attending the University, then vaguely looking for a clerical job— little indeed is known of his activities beyond such trivialities as can be deduced from the general trends of his set. A passage in the correspondence of the famous poet Nekrasov, who happened to meet him once in a bookshop, conveys the image of a sulky, unbalanced, "clumsy and fierce" young man with "the eyes of a child and the shoulders of a furniture mover."

He is also mentioned in a police report as "conversing in low tones with two other students" in a coffeehouse on Nevsky Avenue. And his sister, who married a merchant from Riga, is said to have deplored the poet's emotional adventures with seamstresses and washerwomen. In the autumn of 1849 he visited his father with the special intent of obtaining money for a trip to Spain. His father, a man of simple reactions, slapped him on the face; and a few days later the poor boy was drowned while bathing in the neighboring river. His clothes and a half-eaten apple were found lying under a birch tree, but the body was never recovered.

His fame was sluggish: a passage from the *Georgian Nights,* always the same one, in all anthologies; a violent article by the radical critic Dobrolubov, in 1859, lauding the revolutionary innuendoes of his weakest poems; a general notion in the eighties that a reactionary atmosphere had thwarted and finally destroyed a fine if somewhat inarticulate talent—this was about all.

In the nineties, because of a healthier interest in poetry, coinciding as it sometimes does with a sturdy and dull political era, a flurry of rediscovery started around Perov's rhymes while, on the other hand, the liberal-minded were not averse to following Dobrolubov's cue. The subscription for a monument in one of the public parks proved a perfect success. A leading publisher collected all the scraps of information available in regard to Perov's life and issued his complete works in one fairly plump volume. The monthlies contributed several scholarly surveys. The commemorative meeting in one of the best halls of the capital attracted a crowd.

2

A few minutes before the start, while the speakers were still assembled in a committee room behind the stage, the door opened gustily and there entered a sturdy old man, clad in a frock coat that had seen—on his or on somebody else's shoulders—better times. Without paying the slightest heed to the admonishments of a couple of ribbon-badged University students who, in their capacity of attendants, were attempting to restrain him, he proceeded with perfect dignity towards the committee, bowed, and said, "I am Perov."

A friend of mine, almost twice my age and now the only surviving witness of the event, tells me that the chairman (who as a newspaper editor had a great deal of experience in the matter of extravagant intruders) said without even looking up, "Kick him out." Nobody did—perhaps because one is apt to show a certain courtesy to an old gentleman who is supposedly very drunk. He sat down at the table and, selecting the mildest-looking person, Slavsky, a translator of Longfellow, Heine, and Sully-Prudhomme (and later a member of the terrorist group), asked in a matter-of-fact tone whether the "monument money" had already been collected, and if so, when could he have it.

All the accounts agree on the singularly quiet way in which he made his claim. He did not press his point. He merely stated it as if absolutely unconscious of any possibility of his being disbelieved. What impressed one was that at the very beginning of that weird affair, in that secluded room, among those distinguished men, there he was with his patriarchal beard, faded brown eyes, and potato nose, sedately inquiring about the benefits from the proceedings without even bothering to produce such proofs as might have been faked by an ordinary impostor.

"Are you a relative?" asked someone.

"My name is Konstantin Konstantinovich Perov," said the old man patiently. "I am given to understand that a descendant of my family is in the hall, but that is neither here nor there."

"How old are you?" asked Slavsky.

"I am seventy-four," he replied, "and the victim of several poor crops in succession."

"You are surely aware," remarked the actor Yermakov, "that the poet whose memory we are celebrating tonight was drowned in the river Oredezh exactly fifty years ago."

"*Vzdor*—nonsense," retorted the old man. "I staged that business for reasons of my own."

"And now, my dear fellow," said the chairman, "I really think you must go."

They dismissed him from their consciousness and flocked out onto the severely lighted platform where another committee table, draped in solemn red cloth, with the necessary number of chairs behind it, had been hypnotizing the audience for some time with the glint of its traditional decanter. To the left of this, one could admire the oil painting loaned by the Sheremetevski Art Gallery: it represented Perov at twenty-two, a swarthy young man with romantic hair and an open shirt collar. The picture stand was piously camouflaged by means of leaves and flowers. A lectern with another decanter loomed in front and a grand piano was waiting in the wings to be rolled in later for the musical part of the program.

The hall was well packed with literary people, enlightened lawyers, schoolteachers, scholars, eager university students of both sexes, and the like. A few humble agents of the secret police had been delegated to attend the meeting in inconspicuous spots of the hall, as the government knew by experience that the most staid cultural assemblies had a queer knack of slipping into an orgy of revolutionary propaganda. The fact that one of Perov's first poems contained a veiled but benevolent allusion to the insurrection of 1825 suggested taking certain precautions: one never could tell what might happen after a public mouthing of such lines as "the gloomy sough of Siberian larches communicates with the underground ore—*sibirskikh pikht oogrewmyi shorokh s podzemnoy snositsa roodoy.*"

As one of the accounts has it, "soon one became aware that something vaguely resembling a Dostoyevskian row [the author is thinking of a famous slapstick chapter in *The Possessed*] was creating an atmosphere of awkwardness and suspense." This was due to the fact that the old gentleman deliberately followed the seven members of the jubilee committee onto the platform and then attempted to sit down with them at the table. The chairman, being mainly intent upon avoiding a scuffle in full view of the audience, did his best to make him desist. Under the public disguise of a polite smile he whispered to the patriarch that he would have him ejected from the hall if he did not let go the back of the chair which Slavsky, with a nonchalant air but with a grip of iron, was covertly wresting from under the old man's gnarled hand. The old man refused but lost his hold and was left without a seat. He glanced around, noticed the piano stool in the wings and coolly pulled it onto the stage just a fraction of a second before the hands of a screened attendant tried to snatch it back. He seated himself at some distance from the table and immediately became exhibit number one.

Here the committee made the fatal mistake of again dismissing his presence from their minds: they were, let it be repeated, particularly anxious to avoid a scene; and moreover, the blue hydrangea next to the picture stand half concealed the obnoxious party from their physical vision. Unfortunately, the old gentleman was most conspicuous to the audience, as he sat there on his unseemly pedestal (with its rotatory potentialities hinted at by a recurrent creaking), opening his spectacle case and breathing fishlike upon his glasses, perfectly calm and comfortable, his

venerable head, shabby black clothes, and elastic-sided
boots simultaneously suggesting the needy Russian professor and the prosperous Russian undertaker.

The chairman went up to the lectern and launched upon
his introductory speech. Whisperings rippled all over the
audience, for people were naturally curious to know who
the old fellow was. Firmly bespectacled, with his hands on
his knees, he peered sideways at the portrait, then turned
away from it and inspected the front row. Answering
glances could not help shuttling between the shiny dome
of his head and the curly head of the portrait, for during
the chairman's long speech the details of the intrusion
spread, and the imagination of some started to toy with
the idea that a poet belonging to an almost legendary
period, snugly relegated to it by textbooks, an anachronistic
creature, a live fossil in the nets of an ignorant fisherman,
a kind of Rip van Winkle, was actually attending in his drab
dotage the reunion dedicated to the glory of his youth.

". . . let the name of Perov," said the chairman, ending
his speech, "be never forgotten by thinking Russia. Tyutchev has said that Pushkin will always be remembered by
our country as a first love. In regard to Perov we may say
that he was Russia's first experience in freedom. To a superficial observer this freedom may seem limited to Perov's
phenomenal lavishness of poetical images which appeal
more to the artist than to the citizen. But we, representatives of a more sober generation, are inclined to decipher for
ourselves a deeper, more vital, more human, and more
social sense in such lines of his as

"When the last snow hides in the shade of the cemetery
   wall
 and the coat of my neighbor's black horse
 shows a swift blue sheen in the swift April sun,

45

and the puddles are as many heavens cupped
  in the Negro-hands of the Earth,
then my heart goes out in its tattered cloak
to visit the poor, the blind, the foolish,
the round backs slaving for the round bellies,
all those whose eyes dulled by care or lust do not see
the holes in the snow, the blue horse, the miraculous
  puddle."

A burst of applause greeted this, but all of a sudden there was a break in the clapping, and then disharmonious gusts of laughter; for, as the chairman, still vibrating with the words he had just uttered, went back to the table, the bearded stranger got up and acknowledged the applause by means of jerky nods and awkward wavings of the hand, his expression combining formal gratitude with a certain impatience. Slavsky and a couple of attendants made a desperate attempt to bundle him away, but from the depth of the audience there arose the cries of "Shame, shame!" and *"Astavte starika*—Leave the old man alone!"

I find in one of the accounts the suggestion that there were accomplices among the audience, but I think that mass compassion, which may come as unexpectedly as mass vindictiveness, is sufficient to explain the turn things were taking. In spite of having to cope with three men the "starik" managed to retain a remarkable dignity of demeanor, and when his halfhearted assailants retired and he retrieved the piano stool that had been knocked down during the struggle, there was a murmur of satisfaction. However, the regrettable fact remained that the atmosphere of the meeting was hopelessly impaired. The younger and rowdier members of the audience were beginning to enjoy themselves hugely. The chairman, his nostrils quivering, poured himself out a tumbler of water. Two secret agents were cautiously exchanging glances from two different points of the house.

3

The speech of the chairman was followed by the treasurer's account of the sums received from various institutions and private persons for the erection of a Perov monument in one of the suburban parks. The old man unhurriedly produced a bit of paper and a stubby pencil and, propping the paper on his knee, began to check the figures which were being mentioned. Then the granddaughter of Perov's sister appeared for a moment on the stage. The organizers had had some trouble with this item of the program since the person in question, a fat, popeyed, wax-pale young woman, was being treated for melancholia in a home for mental patients. With twisted mouth and all dressed up in pathetic pink, she was shown to the audience for a moment and then whisked back into the firm hands of a buxom woman delegated by the home.

When Yermakov, who in those days was the darling of theatergoers, a kind of "beau ténor" in terms of the drama, began delivering in his chocolate-cream voice the Prince's speech from the *Georgian Nights*, it became clear that even his best fans were more interested in the reactions of the old man than in the beauty of the delivery. At the lines

> If metal is immortal, then somewhere
> there lies the burnished button that I lost
> upon my seventh birthday in a garden.
> Find me that button and my soul will know
> that every soul is saved and stored and treasured

47

a chink appeared for the first time in his composure and he slowly unfolded a large handkerchief and lustily blew his nose—a sound which sent Yermakov's heavily adumbrated, diamond-bright eye squinting like that of a timorous steed.

The handkerchief was returned to the folds of the coat and only several seconds *after* this did it become noticeable to the people in the first row that tears were trickling from under his glasses. He did not attempt to wipe them, though once or twice his hand did go up to his spectacles with claw-wise spread fingers, but it dropped again, as if by any such gesture (and this was the culminating point of the whole delicate masterpiece) he was afraid to attract attention to his tears. The tremendous applause that followed the recitation was certainly more a tribute to the old man's performance than to the poem in Yermakov's rendering. Then, as soon as the applause petered out, he stood up and marched towards the edge of the platform.

There was no attempt on the part of the committee to stop him, and this for two reasons. First, the chairman, driven to exasperation by the old man's conspicuous behavior, had gone out for a moment and given a certain order. In the second place, a medley of strange doubts was beginning to unnerve some of the organizers, so that there was a complete hush when the old man placed his elbows on the reading stand.

"And this is fame," he said in such a husky voice that from the back rows there came cries of "*Gromche, gromche* —Louder, louder!"

"I am saying that this is fame," he repeated, grimly peering over his spectacles at the audience. "A score of frivolous poems, words made to joggle and jingle, and a man's name is remembered as if he had been of some use to humanity! No, gentlemen, do not delude yourselves. Our empire and the throne of our father the Tsar still stand as they stood, akin to frozen thunder in their invulnerable might, and the misguided youth who scribbled rebellious verse half a century ago is now a law-abiding old man respected by honest citizens. An old man, let me add, who needs your protection. I am the victim of the elements: the land I had plowed with my sweat, the lambs I had personally suckled, the wheat I had seen waving its golden arms—"

It was then that two enormous policemen quickly and painlessly removed the old man. The audience had a glimpse of his being rushed out—his dickey protruding one way, his beard the other, a cuff dangling from his wrist, but still that gravity and that pride in his eyes.

When reporting the celebration, the leading dailies referred only in passing to the "regrettable incident" that had marred it. But the disreputable St. Petersburg Record, a lurid and reactionary rag edited by the brothers Kherstov for the benefit of the lower middle class and of a blissfully semiliterate substratum of working people, blazed forth with a series of articles maintaining that the "regrettable incident" was nothing less than the reappearance of the authentic Perov.

4

In the meantime, the old man had been collected by the very wealthy and vulgarly eccentric merchant Gromov, whose household was full of vagabond monks, quack doctors, and "pogromystics." The Record printed interviews with the impostor. In these the latter said dreadful things about the "lackeys of the revolutionary party" who had cheated him of his identity and robbed him of his money. This money he proposed to obtain by law from the publishers of Perov's complete works. A drunken scholar attached to the Gromov household pointed out the (unfortunately rather striking) similarity between the old man's features and those of the portrait.

There appeared a detailed but most implausible account of his having staged a suicide in order to lead a Christian life in the bosom of Saint Russia. He had been everything: a peddler, a bird catcher, a ferryman on the Volga, and had wound up by acquiring a bit of land in a remote province. I have seen a copy of a sordid-looking booklet, *The Death and Resurrection of Konstantin Perov,* which used to be sold on the streets by shivering beggars, together with the *Adventures of the Marquis de Sade* and the *Memoirs of an Amazon.*

My best find, however, in looking through old files, is a smudgy photograph of the bearded impostor perched upon the marble of the unfinished Perov monument in a leafless park. He is seen standing very straight with his arms folded; he wears a round fur cap and a new pair of galoshes but no overcoat; a little crowd of his backers is gathered at his feet, and their little white faces stare into the camera with that special navel-eyed, self-complacent expression peculiar to old pictures of lynching parties.

Given this atmosphere of florid hooliganism and reactionary smugness (so closely linked up with governmental ideas in Russia, no matter whether the Tsar be called Alexander, Nicholas, or Joe), the intelligentsia could hardly bear to visualize the disaster of identifying the pure, ardent, revolutionary-minded Perov as represented by his poems with a vulgar old man wallowing in a painted pigsty. The tragic part was that while neither Gromov nor the Kherstov brothers really believed the purveyor of their fun was the true Perov, many honest, cultivated people had become

obsessed by the impossible thought that what they had
ejected was Truth and Justice.

As a recently published letter from Slavsky to Korolenko
has it: "One shudders to think that a gift of destiny unparal-
leled in history, the Lazaruslike resurrection of a great poet
of the past, may be ungratefully ignored—nay, even more,
deemed a fiendish deceit on the part of a man whose only
crime has been half a century of silence and a few minutes
of wild talk." The wording is muddled but the gist is clear:
intellectual Russia was less afraid of falling victim to a hoax
than of sponsoring a hideous blunder. But there was something she was still more afraid of, and that was the destruc-
tion of an ideal; for your radical is ready to upset everything
in the world except any such trivial bauble, no matter how
doubtful and dusty, that for some reason radicalism has
enshrined.

It is rumored that at a certain secret session of the Society
for the Advancement of Russian Literature the numerous
insulting epistles that the old man kept sending in were
carefully compared by experts with a very old letter written
by the poet in his teens. It had been discovered in a certain
private archive, was believed to be the only sample of
Perov's hand, and none except the scholars who pored over
its faded ink knew of its existence. Neither do we know
what their findings were.

It is further rumored that a lump of money was amassed
and that the old man was approached without the knowledge of his disgraceful companions. Apparently, a sub-
stantial monthly pension was to be granted him under the
condition that he return at once to his farm and stay there
in decorous silence and oblivion. Apparently, too, the offer
was accepted, for he vanished as jerkily as he had appeared,
while Gromov consoled himself for the loss of his pet by

adopting a shady hypnotizer of French extraction who a year or two later was to enjoy some success at the Court.

The monument was duly unveiled and became a great favorite with the local pigeons. The sales of the collected works fizzled out genteelly in the middle of a fourth edition. Finally, a few years later, in the region where Perov had been born, the oldest though not necessarily the brightest inhabitant told a lady journalist that he remembered his father telling him of finding a skeleton in a reedy part of the river.

5

This would have been all had not the revolution come, turning up slabs of rich earth together with the white rootlets of little plants and fat mauve worms which otherwise would have remained buried. When, in the early twenties, in the dark, hungry, but morbidly active city, various odd cultural institutions sprouted (such as bookshops where famous but destitute writers sold their own books, and so on), somebody or other earned a couple of months' living by arranging a little Perov museum, and this led to yet another resurrection.

The exhibits? All of them except one (the letter). A second-hand past in a shabby hall. The oval-shaped eyes and brown locks of the precious Sheremetevsky portrait (with a crack in the region of the open collar suggesting a tentative beheading); a battered volume of the *Georgian Nights* that was thought to have belonged to Nekrasov; an indifferent photograph of the village school built on the spot where the poet's father had owned a house and an orchard. An old glove that some visitor to the museum had forgotten. Several editions of Perov's works distributed in such a way as to occupy the greatest possible space.

And because all these poor relics still refused to form a happy family, several period articles had been added, such as the dressing gown that a famous radical critic had worn in his rococo study, and the chains he had worn in his wooden Siberian prison. But there again, since neither this nor the portraits of various writers of the time were bulky enough, a model of the first railway train to run in Russia (in the forties, between St. Petersburg and Tsarskoye selo) had been installed in the middle of that dismal room.

The old man, now well over ninety but still articulate in speech and reasonably erect in carriage, would show you around the place as if he were your host instead of being the janitor. One had the odd impression that presently he would lead you into the next (non-existing) room, where supper would be served. All that he really possessed, however, was a stove behind a screen and the bench on which he slept; but if you bought one of the books exhibited for sale at the entrance he would autograph it for you as a matter of course.

Then one morning he was found dead on his bench by the woman who brought him his food. Three quarrelsome families lived for a while in the museum, and soon nothing remained of its contents. And as if some great hand with a great rasping sound had torn out a great bunch of pages from a number of books, or as if some frivolous story writer had bottled an imp of fiction in the vessel of truth, or as if. . . .

But no matter. Somehow or other, in the next twenty years or so, Russia lost all contact with Perov's poetry. Young Soviet citizens know as little about his works as they do about mine. No doubt a time will come when he will be republished and readmired; still, one cannot help feeling that, as things stand, people are missing a great deal. One wonders also what future historians will make of the old man and his extraordinary contention. But that, of course, is a matter of secondary importance.

Boston, 1944.

First Love

1

In the early years of this century, a travel agency on Nevski Avenue displayed a three-foot-long model of an oak-brown international sleeping car. In delicate verisimilitude it completely outranked the painted tin of my clockwork trains. Unfortunately it was not for sale. One could make out the blue upholstery inside, the embossed leather lining of the compartment walls, their polished panels, inset mirrors, tulip-shaped reading lamps, and other maddening details. Spacious windows alternated with narrower ones, single or geminate, and some of these were of frosted glass. In a few of the compartments, the beds had been made.

The then great and glamorous Nord Express (it was never the same after World War I), consisting solely of such international cars and running but twice a week, connected St. Petersburg with Paris. I would have said: directly with Paris, had passengers not been obliged to change from one train to a superficially similar one at the Russo-German frontier (Verzhbolovo-Eydtkuhnen), where the ample and lazy Russian sixty-and-a-half-inch gauge was replaced by the fifty-six-and-a-half-inch standard of Europe and coal succeeded birch logs.

In the far end of my mind I can unravel, I think, at least five such journeys to Paris, with the Riviera or Biarritz as their ultimate destination. In 1909, the year I now single out, my two small sisters had been left at home with nurses and aunts. Wearing gloves and a traveling cap, my father sat reading a book in the compartment he shared with our tutor. My brother and I were separated from them by a washroom. My mother and her maid occupied a compartment adjacent to ours. The odd one of our party, my father's valet, Osip (whom, a decade later, the pedantic Bolsheviks were to shoot, because he appropriated our bicycles instead of turning them over to the nation), had a stranger for companion.

In April of that year, Peary had reached the North Pole. In May, Chaliapin had sung in Paris. In June, bothered by rumors of new and better Zeppelins, the United States War Department had told reporters of plans for an aerial Navy. In July, Blériot had flown from Calais to Dover (with a little additional loop when he lost his bearings). It was late August now. The firs and marshes of northwestern Russia sped by, and on the following day gave way to German pine barrens and heather.

At a collapsible table, my mother and I played a card game called *durachki*. Although it was still broad daylight, our cards, a glass, and on a different plane the locks of a suitcase were reflected in the window. Through forest and field, and in sudden ravines, and among scuttling cottages,

those discarnate gamblers kept steadily playing on for
steadily sparkling stakes.

"*Ne budet-li, ti ved' ustal* [Haven't you had enough,
aren't you tired]?" my mother would ask, and then would
be lost in thought as she slowly shuffled the cards. The door
of the compartment was open and I could see the corridor
window, where the wires—six thin black wires—were doing
their best to slant up, to ascend skywards, despite the
lightning blows dealt them by one telegraph pole after
another; but just as all six, in a triumphant swoop of pathetic elation, were about to reach the top of the window, a
particularly vicious blow would bring them down, as low
as they had ever been, and they would have to start all
over again.

When, on such journeys as these, the train changed its
pace to a dignified amble and all but grazed house fronts
and shop signs, as we passed through some big German
town, I used to feel a twofold excitement, which terminal
stations could not provide. I saw a city with its toylike
trams, linden trees, and brick walls enter the compartment,
hobnob with the mirrors, and fill to the brim the windows
on the corridor side. This informal contact between train
and city was one part of the thrill. The other was putting
myself in the place of some passer-by who, I imagined,
was moved as I would be moved myself to see the long,
romantic, auburn cars, with their intervestibular connecting
curtains as black as bat wings and their metal lettering
copper-bright in the low sun, unhurriedly negotiate an iron
bridge across an everyday thoroughfare and then turn, with
all windows suddenly ablaze, around a last block of houses.

There were drawbacks to those optical amalgamations.
The wide-windowed dining car, a vista of chaste bottles of
mineral water, miter-folded napkins, and dummy choco-

late bars (whose wrappers—Cailler, Kohler, and so forth—enclosed nothing but wood) would be perceived at first as a cool haven beyond a consecution of reeling blue corridors; but as the meal progressed toward its fatal last course, one would keep catching the car in the act of being recklessly sheathed, lurching waiters and all, in the landscape, while the landscape itself went through a complex system of motion, the day-time moon stubbornly keeping abreast of one's plate, the distant meadows opening fanwise, the near trees sweeping up on invisible swings toward the track, a parallel rail line all at once committing suicide by anastomosis, a bank of nictitating grass rising, rising, rising, until the little witness of mixed velocities was made to disgorge his portion of *omelette aux confitures de fraises*.

It was at night, however, that the *Compagnie Internationale des Wagons-Lits et des Grands Express Européens* lived up to the magic of its name. From my bed under my brother's bunk (Was he asleep? Was he there at all?), in the semidarkness of our compartment, I watched things, and parts of things, and shadows, and sections of shadows cautiously moving about and getting nowhere. The woodwork gently creaked and crackled. Near the door that led to the toilet, a dim garment on a peg and, higher up, the tassel of the blue, bivalved night light swung rhythmically. It was hard to correlate those halting approaches, that hooded stealth, with the headlong rush of the outside night, which I knew *was* rushing by, spark-streaked, illegible.

I would put myself to sleep by the simple act of identifying myself with the engine driver. A sense of drowsy well-being invaded my veins as soon as I had everything nicely arranged—the carefree passengers in their rooms enjoying the ride I was giving them, smoking, exchanging knowing smiles, nodding, dozing; the waiters and cooks and train guards (whom I had to place somewhere) carousing in the diner; and myself, goggled and begrimed, peering out of the engine cab at the tapering track, at the ruby or emerald point in the black distance. And then, in my sleep, I would see something totally different—a glass marble rolling under a grand piano or a toy engine lying on its side with its wheels still working gamely.

A change in the speed of the train sometimes interrupted the current of my sleep. Slow lights were stalking by; each, in passing, investigated the same chink, and then a luminous compass measured the shadows. Presently, the train stopped with a long-drawn Westinghousian sigh. Something (my brother's spectacles, as it proved next day) fell from above. It was marvelously exciting to move to the foot of one's bed, with part of the bedclothes following, in order to undo cautiously the catch of the window shade, which could be made to slide only halfway up, impeded as it was by the edge of the upper berth.

Like moons around Jupiter, pale moths revolved about a lone lamp. A dismembered newspaper stirred on a bench. Somewhere on the train one could hear muffled voices, somebody's comfortable cough. There was nothing particularly interesting in the portion of station platform before me, and still I could not tear myself away from it until it departed of its own accord.

Next morning, wet fields with misshapen willows along the radius of a ditch or a row of poplars afar, traversed by a horizontal band of milky-white mist, told one that the train was spinning through Belgium. It reached Paris at 4 P.M.; and even if the stay was only an overnight one, I had always time to purchase something—say, a little brass *Tour Eiffel*, rather roughly coated with silver paint—before we boarded at noon on the following day the Sud Express, which, on its way to Madrid, dropped us around 10 P.M. at the La Négresse station of Biarritz, a few miles from the Spanish frontier.

2

Biarritz still retained its quiddity in those days. Dusty blackberry bushes and weedy *terrains à vendre* bordered the road that led to our villa. The Carlton was still being built. Some thirty-six years had to elapse before Brigadier General Samuel McCroskey would occupy the royal suite of the Hotel du Palais, which stands on the site of a former palace, where, in the sixties, that incredibly agile medium, Daniel Home, is said to have been caught stroking with his bare foot (in imitation of a ghost hand) the kind, trustful face of Empress Eugénie. On the promenade near the Casino, an elderly flower girl, with carbon eyebrows and a painted smile, nimbly slipped the plump torus of a carnation into the buttonhole of an intercepted stroller whose left jowl accentuated its royal fold as he glanced down sideways at the coy insertion of the flower.

Along the back line of the *plage*, various seaside chairs and stools supported the parents of straw-hatted children who were playing in front on the sand. I could be seen on my knees trying to set a found comb aflame by means of a magnifying glass. Men sported white trousers that to the eye of today would look as if they had comically shrunk in the washing; ladies wore, that particular season, light coats with silk-faced lapels, hats with big crowns and wide brims, dense embroidered white veils, frill-fronted blouses, frills at their wrists, frills on their parasols. The breeze salted one's lips. At a tremendous pace a stray golden-orange butterfly came dashing across the palpitating *plage*.

Additional movement and sound were provided by vendors hawking *cacahuètes*, sugared violets, pistachio ice cream of a heavenly green, cachou pellets, and huge convex pieces of dry, gritty, waferlike stuff that came from a red barrel. With a distinctness that no later superpositions have dimmed, I see that waffleman stomp along through deep mealy sand, with the heavy cask on his bent back. When called, he would sling it off his shoulder by a twist of its strap, bang it down on the sand in a Tower of Pisa position, wipe his face with his sleeve, and proceed to manipulate a kind of arrow-and-dial arrangement with numbers on the lid of the cask. The arrow rasped and whirred around. Luck was supposed to fix the size of a sou's worth of wafer. The bigger the piece, the more I was sorry for him.

The process of bathing took place on another part of the beach. Professional bathers, burly Basques in black bathing suits, were there to help ladies and children enjoy the terrors of the surf. Such a *baigneur* would place you with your back to the incoming wave and hold you by the hand as the rising, rotating mass of foamy, green water violently descended upon you from behind, knocking you off your feet with one mighty wallop. After a dozen of these tumbles, the *baigneur*, glistening like a seal, would lead his panting, shivering, moistly snuffling charge landward, to the flat foreshore, where an unforgettable old woman with gray hairs on her chin promptly chose a bathing robe from several hanging on a clothesline. In the security of a little cabin, one would be helped by yet another attendant to peel off one's soggy, sand-heavy bathing suit. It would plop onto the boards, and, still shivering, one would step out of it and trample on its bluish, diffuse stripes. The cabin smelt of pine. The attendant, a hunchback with beaming wrinkles, brought a basin of steaming-hot water, in which one immersed one's feet. From him I learned, and have preserved ever since in a glass cell of my memory, that "butterfly" in the Basque language is *misericoletea*—or at least it sounded so (among the seven words I have found in dictionaries the closest approach is *micheletea*).

3

On the browner and wetter part of the *plage*, that part which at low tide yielded the best mud for castles, I found myself digging, one day, side by side with a little French girl called Colette.

She would be ten in November, I had been ten in April. Attention was drawn to a jagged bit of violet mussel shell upon which she had stepped with the bare sole of her narrow long-toed foot. No, I was not English. Her greenish eyes seemed flecked with the overflow of the freckles that covered her sharp-featured face. She wore what might now be termed a playsuit, consisting of a blue jersey with rolled-up sleeves and blue knitted shorts. I had taken her at first for a boy and then had been puzzled by the bracelet on her thin wrist and the corkscrew brown curls dangling from under her sailor cap.

She spoke in birdlike bursts of rapid twitter, mixing governess English and Parisian French. Two years before, on the same *plage,* I had been much attached to the lovely, sun-tanned little daughter of a Serbian physician; but when I met Colette, I knew at once that this was the real thing. Colette seemed to me so much stranger than all my other chance playmates at Biarritz! I somehow acquired the feeling that she was less happy than I, less loved. A bruise on her delicate, downy forearm gave rise to awful conjectures. "He pinches as bad as my mummy," she said, speaking of a crab. I evolved various schemes to save her from her parents, who were "*des bourgeois de Paris*" as I heard somebody tell my mother with a slight shrug. I interpreted the disdain in my own fashion, as I knew that those people had come all the way from Paris in their blue-and-yellow limousine (a fashionable adventure in those days) but had drably sent Colette with her dog and governess by an ordinary coach train. The dog was a female fox terrier with bells on her collar and a most waggly behind. From sheer exuberance, she would lap up salt water out of Colette's toy pail. I remember the sail, the sunset, and the lighthouse pictured on that pail, but I cannot recall the dog's name, and this bothers me.

During the two months of our stay at Biarritz, my passion for Colette all but surpassed my passion for butterflies. Since my parents were not keen to meet hers, I saw her only on the beach; but I thought of her constantly. If I noticed she had been crying, I felt a surge of helpless anguish that brought tears to my own eyes. I could not destroy the mosquitoes that had left their bites on her frail neck, but I could, and did, have a successful fist fight with a red-haired boy who had been rude to her. She used to give me warm handfuls of hard candy. One day, as we were bending together over a starfish, and Colette's ringlets were tickling my ear, she suddenly turned toward me and kissed me on the cheek. So great was my emotion that all I could think of saying was, "You little monkey."

I had a gold coin that I assumed would pay for our elopement. Where did I want to take her? Spain? America? The mountains above Pau? "*Là-bas, là-bas, dans la montagne*," as I had heard Carmen sing at the opera. One strange night, I lay awake, listening to the recurrent thud of the ocean and planning our flight. The ocean seemed to rise and grope in the darkness and then heavily fall on its face.

Of our actual getaway, I have little to report. My memory retains a glimpse of her obediently putting on rope-soled canvas shoes, on the lee side of a flapping tent, while I stuffed a folding butterfly net into a brown paper bag. The next glimpse is of our evading pursuit by entering a pitch-dark *cinéma* near the Casino (which, of course, was absolutely out of bounds). There we sat, holding hands across the dog, which now and then gently jingled in Colette's lap, and were shown a jerky, drizzly, but highly exciting bullfight at St. Sebástian. My final glimpse is of myself being led along the promenade by my tutor. His long legs move with a kind of ominous briskness and I can see the muscles of his grimly set jaw working under the tight skin. My bespectacled brother, aged nine, whom he happens to hold with his other hand, keeps trotting out forward to peer at me with awed curiosity, like a little owl.

Among the trivial souvenirs acquired at Biarritz before leaving, my favorite was not the small bull of black stone and not the sonorous sea shell but something which now seems almost symbolic—a meerschaum penholder with a tiny peephole of crystal in its ornamental part. One held it quite close to one's eye, screwing up the other, and when one had got rid of the shimmer of one's own lashes, a miraculous photographic view of the bay and of the line of cliffs ending in a lighthouse could be seen inside.

And now a delightful thing happens. The process of re-creating that penholder and the microcosm in its eyelet stimulates my memory to a last effort. I try again to recall the name of Colette's dog—and, sure enough, along those remote beaches, over the glossy evening sands of the past, where each footprint slowly fills up with sunset water, here it comes, here it comes, echoing and vibrating: Floss, Floss, Floss!

Colette was back in Paris by the time we stopped there for a day before continuing our homeward journey; and there, in a fawn park under a cold blue sky, I saw her (by arrangement between our mentors, I believe) for the last time. She carried a hoop and a short stick to drive it with, and everything about her was extremely proper and stylish in an autumnal, Parisian, *tenue-de-ville-pour-fillettes* way. She took from her governess and slipped into my brother's hand a farewell present, a box of sugar-coated almonds, meant, I knew, solely for me; and instantly she was off, tap-tapping her glinting hoop through light and shade, around and around a fountain choked with dead leaves near which I stood. The leaves mingle in my memory with the leather of her shoes and gloves, and there was, I remember, some detail in her attire (perhaps a ribbon on her Scottish cap, or the pattern of her stockings) that reminded me then of the rainbow spiral in a glass marble. I still seem to be holding that wisp of iridescence, not knowing exactly where to fit it, while she runs with her hoop ever faster around me and finally dissolves among the slender shadows cast on the graveled path by the interlaced arches of its low looped fence.

Boston, 1948.

Signs and Symbols

1

For the fourth time in as many years they were confronted
with the problem of what birthday present to bring a young
man who was incurably deranged in his mind. He had no
desires. Man-made objects were to him either hives of evil,
vibrant with a malignant activity that he alone could perceive, or gross comforts for which no use could be found in
his abstract world. After eliminating a number of articles
that might offend him or frighten him (anything in the
gadget line for instance was taboo), his parents chose a
dainty and innocent trifle: a basket with ten different fruit
jellies in ten little jars.

At the time of his birth they had been married already
for a long time; a score of years had elapsed, and now they
were quite old. Her drab gray hair was done anyhow. She
wore cheap black dresses. Unlike other women of her age

(such as Mrs. Sol, their next-door neighbor, whose face was all pink and mauve with paint and whose hat was a cluster of brookside flowers), she presented a naked white countenance to the fault-finding light of spring days. Her husband, who in the old country had been a fairly successful businessman, was now wholly dependent on his brother Isaac, a real American of almost forty years standing. They seldom saw him and had nicknamed him "the Prince."

That Friday everything went wrong. The underground train lost its life current between two stations, and for a quarter of an hour one could hear nothing but the dutiful beating of one's heart and the rustling of newspapers. The bus they had to take next kept them waiting for ages; and when it did come, it was crammed with garrulous high-school children. It was raining hard as they walked up the brown path leading to the sanitarium. There they waited again; and instead of their boy shuffling into the room as he usually did (his poor face blotched with acne, ill-shaven, sullen, and confused), a nurse they knew, and did not care for, appeared at last and brightly explained that he had again attempted to take his life. He was all right, she said, but a visit might disturb him. The place was so miserably understaffed, and things got mislaid or mixed up so easily, that they decided not to leave their present in the office but to bring it to him next time they came.

She waited for her husband to open his umbrella and then took his arm. He kept clearing his throat in a special resonant way he had when he was upset. They reached the bus-stop shelter on the other side of the street and he closed his umbrella. A few feet away, under a swaying and dripping tree, a tiny half-dead unfledged bird was helplessly twitching in a puddle.

During the long ride to the subway station, she and her

husband did not exchange a word; and every time she glanced at his old hands (swollen veins, brown-spotted skin), clasped and twitching upon the handle of his umbrella, she felt the mounting pressure of tears. As she looked around trying to hook her mind onto something, it gave her a kind of soft shock, a mixture of compassion and wonder, to notice that one of the passengers, a girl with dark hair and grubby red toenails, was weeping on the shoulder of an older woman. Whom did that woman resemble? She resembled Rebecca Borisovna, whose daughter had married one of the Soloveichiks—in Minsk, years ago.

The last time he had tried to do it, his method had been, in the doctor's words, a masterpiece of inventiveness; he would have succeeded, had not an envious fellow patient thought he was learning to fly—and stopped him. What he really wanted to do was to tear a hole in his world and escape.

The system of his delusions had been the subject of an elaborate paper in a scientific monthly, but long before that she and her husband had puzzled it out for themselves. "Referential mania," Herman Brink had called it. In these very rare cases the patient imagines that everything happening around him is a veiled reference to his personality and existence. He excludes real people from the conspiracy —because he considers himself to be so much more intelligent than other men. Phenomenal nature shadows him wherever he goes. Clouds in the staring sky transmit to one another, by means of slow signs, incredibly detailed information regarding him. His inmost thoughts are discussed at nightfall, in manual alphabet, by darkly gesticulating trees. Pebbles or stains or sun flecks form patterns representing in some awful way messages which he must intercept. Everything is a cipher and of everything he is the theme. Some of the spies are detached observers, such are glass surfaces and still pools; others, such as coats in store windows, are prejudiced witnesses, lynchers at heart; others again (running water, storms) are hysterical to the point of insanity, have a distorted opinion of him and grotesquely misinterpret his actions. He must be always on his guard and devote every minute and module of life to the decoding of the undulation of things. The very air he exhales is indexed and filed away. If only the interest he provokes were limited to his immediate surroundings—but alas it is not! With distance the torrents of wild scandal increase in volume and volubility. The silhouettes of his blood corpuscles, magnified a million times, flit over vast plains; and still farther, great mountains of unbearable solidity and height sum up in terms of granite and groaning firs the ultimate truth of his being.

2

When they emerged from the thunder and foul air of the subway, the last dregs of the day were mixed with the street lights. She wanted to buy some fish for supper, so she handed him the basket of jelly jars, telling him to go home. He walked up to the third landing and then remembered he had given her his keys earlier in the day.

In silence he sat down on the steps and in silence rose when some ten minutes later she came, heavily trudging upstairs, wanly smiling, shaking her head in deprecation of her silliness. They entered their two-room flat and he at once went to the mirror. Straining the corners of his mouth apart by means of his thumbs, with a horrible masklike grimace, he removed his new hopelessly uncomfortable dental plate and severed the long tusks of saliva connecting him to it. He read his Russian-language newspaper while she laid the table. Still reading, he ate the pale victuals that needed no teeth. She knew his moods and was also silent.

When he had gone to bed, she remained in the living room with her pack of soiled cards and her old albums. Across the narrow yard where the rain tinkled in the dark against some battered ash cans, windows were blandly alight and in one of them a black-trousered man with his bare elbows raised could be seen lying supine on an untidy bed. She pulled the blind down and examined the photographs. As a baby he looked more surprised than most babies. From a fold in the album, a German maid they had had in Leipzig and her fat-faced fiancé fell out. Minsk, the Revolution, Leipzig, Berlin, Leipzig, a slanting house front badly out of focus. Four years old, in a park: moodily, shyly, with puckered forehead, looking away from an eager squirrel as he would from any other stranger. Aunt Rosa, a fussy, angular, wild-eyed old lady, who had lived in a tremulous world of bad news, bankruptcies, train accidents, cancerous growths—until the Germans put her to death, together with all the people she had worried about. Age six—that was when he drew wonderful birds with human hands and feet, and suffered from insomnia like a grown-up man. His cousin, now a famous chess player. He again, aged about eight, already difficult to understand, afraid of the wallpaper in the passage, afraid of a certain picture in a book which merely showed an idyllic landscape with rocks on a hillside and an old cart wheel hanging from the branch of a leafless tree. Aged ten: the year they left Europe. The shame, the pity, the humiliating difficulties, the ugly, vicious, backward children he was with in that special school. And then came a time in his life, coinciding with a long convalescence after pneumonia, when those little phobias of his which his parents had stubbornly regarded as the eccentricities of a prodigiously gifted child hardened as it were into a dense tangle of logically interacting illusions, making him totally inaccessible to normal minds.

This, and much more, she accepted—for after all living did mean accepting the loss of one joy after another, not even joys in her case—mere possibilities of improvement. She thought of the endless waves of pain that for some reason or other she and her husband had to endure; of the invisible giants hurting her boy in some unimaginable fashion; of the incalculable amount of tenderness contained in the world; of the fate of this tenderness, which is either crushed, or wasted, or transformed into madness; of neglected children humming to themselves in unswept corners; of beautiful weeds that cannot hide from the farmer and helplessly have to watch the shadow of his simian stoop leave mangled flowers in its wake, as the monstrous darkness approaches.

3

It was past midnight when from the living room she heard her husband moan; and presently he staggered in, wearing over his nightgown the old overcoat with astrakhan collar which he much preferred to the nice blue bathrobe he had.

"I can't sleep," he cried.

"Why," she asked, "why can't you sleep? You were so tired."

"I can't sleep because I am dying," he said and lay down on the couch.

"Is it your stomach? Do you want me to call Dr. Solov?"

"No doctors, no doctors," he moaned, "To the devil with doctors! We must get him out of there quick. Otherwise we'll be responsible. Responsible!" he repeated and hurled himself into a sitting position, both feet on the floor, thumping his forehead with his clenched fist.

"All right," she said quietly, "we shall bring him home tomorrow morning."

"I would like some tea," said her husband and retired to the bathroom.

Bending with difficulty, she retrieved some playing cards and a photograph or two that had slipped from the couch to the floor: knave of hearts, nine of spades, ace of spades, Elsa and her bestial beau.

He returned in high spirits, saying in a loud voice:

"I have it all figured out. We will give him the bedroom. Each of us will spend part of the night near him and the other part on this couch. By turns. We will have the doctor see him at least twice a week. It does not matter what the Prince says. He won't have to say much anyway because it will come out cheaper."

The telephone rang. It was an unusual hour for their telephone to ring. His left slipper had come off and he groped for it with his heel and toe as he stood in the middle of the room, and childishly, toothlessly, gaped at his wife. Having more English than he did, it was she who attended to calls.

"Can I speak to Charlie," said a girl's dull little voice.

"What number you want? No. That is not the right number."

The receiver was gently cradled. Her hand went to her old tired heart.

"It frightened me," she said.

He smiled a quick smile and immediately resumed his excited monologue. They would fetch him as soon as it was day. Knives would have to be kept in a locked drawer. Even at his worst he presented no danger to other people.

The telephone rang a second time. The same toneless anxious young voice asked for Charlie.

"You have the incorrect number. I will tell you what you are doing: you are turning the letter O instead of the zero."

They sat down to their unexpected festive midnight tea. The birthday present stood on the table. He sipped noisily; his face was flushed; every now and then he imparted a circular motion to his raised glass so as to make the sugar dissolve more thoroughly. The vein on the side of his bald head where there was a large birthmark stood out conspicuously and, although he had shaved that morning, a silvery bristle showed on his chin. While she poured him another glass of tea, he put on his spectacles and re-examined with pleasure the luminous yellow, green, red little jars. His clumsy moist lips spelled out their eloquent labels: apricot, grape, beech plum, quince. He had got to crab apple, when the telephone rang again.

Boston, 1948.

The Assistant Producer

1

Meaning? Well, because sometimes life is merely that—an Assistant Producer. Tonight we shall go to the movies. Back to the Thirties, and down the Twenties, and round the corner to the old Europe Picture Palace. She was a celebrated singer. Not opera, not even *Cavalleria Rusticana*, not anything like that. "La Slavska"—that is what the French called her. Style: one-tenth *tzigane*, one-seventh Russian peasant girl (she had been that herself originally), and five-ninths popular—and by popular I mean a hodgepodge of artificial folklore, military melodrama, and official patriotism. The fraction left unfilled seems sufficient to represent the physical splendor of her prodigious voice.

Coming from what was, geographically at least, the very heart of Russia, it eventually reached the big cities, Moscow, St. Petersburg, and the Tsar's milieu where that sort of style was greatly appreciated. In Feodor Chaliapin's dressing room there hung a photograph of her: Russian headgear with pearls, hand propping cheek, dazzling teeth between fleshy lips, and a great clumsy scrawl right across: "For you, Fedyusha." Stars of snow, each revealing, before the edges melted, its complex symmetry, would gently come to rest on the shoulders and sleeves and mustaches and caps—all waiting in a queue for the box office to open. Up to her very death she treasured above all—or pretended to do so—a fancy medal and a huge brooch that had been given her by the Tsarina. They came from the firm of jewelers which used to do such profitable business by presenting the Imperial couple on every festive occasion with this or that emblem (each year increasing in worth) of massive Tsardom: some great lump of amethyst with a ruby-studded bronze troika stranded on top like Noah's Ark on Mount Ararat, or a sphere of crystal the size of a watermelon surmounted by a gold eagle with square diamond eyes very much like those of Rasputin (many years later some of the less symbolic ones were exhibited at a World's Fair by the Soviets as samples of their own thriving Art).

Had things gone on as they were seeming to go, she might have been still singing tonight in a central-heated Hall of Nobility or at Tsarskoye, and I should be turning off her broadcast voice in some remote corner of steppe-mother Siberia. But destiny took the wrong turning; and when the Revolution happened, followed by the War of the Reds and the Whites, her wily peasant soul chose the more practical party.

Ghostly multitudes of ghostly Cossacks on ghost-horseback are seen charging through the fading name of the assistant producer. Then dapper General Golubkov is disclosed idly scanning the battlefield through a pair of opera glasses. When movies and we were young, we used to be shown what the sights divulged neatly framed in two connected circles. Not now. What we do see next is General Golubkov, all indolence suddenly gone, leaping into the saddle, looming sky-high for an instant on his rearing steed and then rocketing into a crazy attack.

But the unexpected is the infra-red in the spectrum of Art: instead of the conditional *ra-ta-ta* reflex of machine gunnery, a woman's voice is heard singing afar. Nearer, still nearer, and finally all-pervading. A gorgeous contralto voice expanding into whatever the musical director found in his files in the way of Russian lilt. Who is this leading the infra-Reds? A woman. The singing spirit of that particular, especially well-trained battalion. Marching in front, trampling the alfalfa and pouring out her Volga-Volga song. Dapper and daring *djighit* Golubkov (now we know what he had descried), although wounded in several spots, manages to snatch her up on the gallop, and, lusciously struggling, she is borne away.

Strangely enough, that vile script was enacted in reality. I myself have known at least two reliable witnesses of the event; and the sentries of history have let it pass unchallenged. Very soon we find her maddening the officers' mess with her dark buxom beauty and wild, wild songs. She was a Belle Dame with a good deal of Merci, and there was a punch about her that Louise von Lenz or the Green Lady lacked. She it was who sweetened the general retreat of the Whites, which began shortly after her magic appearance at General Golubkov's camp. We get a gloomy glimpse of ravens, or crows, or whatever birds proved available, wheeling in the dusk and slowly descending upon a plain littered with bodies somewhere in Ventura County. A White soldier's dead hand is still clutching a medallion with his mother's face. A Red soldier near by has on his shattered breast a letter from home with the same old woman blinking through the dissolving lines.

And then, in traditional contrast, pat comes a mighty burst of music and song with a rhythmic clapping of hands and stamping of booted feet and we see General Golubkov's staff in full revelry—a lithe Georgian dancing with a dagger, the self-conscious samovar reflecting distorted faces, the Slavska throwing her head back with a throaty laugh, and the fat man of the corps, horribly drunk, braided collar undone, greasy lips pursed for a bestial kiss, leaning across the table (close-up of an overturned glass) to hug—nothingness, for wiry and perfectly sober General Golubkov has deftly removed her and now, as they both stand facing the gang, says in a cold, clear voice: "Gentlemen, I want to present you my bride"—and in the stunned silence that follows, a stray bullet from outside chances to shatter the dawn-blue windowpane, after which a roar of applause greets the glamorous couple.

There is little doubt that her capture had not been wholly a fortuitous occurrence. Indeterminism is banned from the studio. It is even less doubtful that when the great exodus began and they, as many others, meandered via Sirkedji to Motzstrasse and Rue Vaugirard, the General and his wife already formed one team, one song, one cipher. Quite naturally he became an efficient member of the W.W. (White Warriors Union), traveling about, organizing military courses for Russian boys, arranging relief concerts, unearthing barracks for the destitute, settling local disputes, and doing all this in a most unobtrusive manner. I suppose it was useful in some ways, that W.W. Unfortunately for its spiritual welfare, it was quite incapable of cutting itself off from monarchist groups abroad and did not feel, as the émigré intelligentsia felt, the dreadful vulgarity, the Ur-Hitlerism of those ludicrous but vicious organizations.

When well-meaning Americans ask me whether I know charming Colonel So-and-so or grand old Count de Kick-offsky, I have not the heart to tell them the dismal truth.

But there was also another type of person connected with the W.W. I am thinking of those adventurous souls who helped the cause by crossing the frontier through some snow-muffled fir forest, to potter about their native land in the various disguises worked out, oddly enough, by the social revolutionaries of yore, and quietly bring back to the little café in Paris called "Esh-Bubliki," or to the little *Kneipe* in Berlin that had no special name, the kind of useful trifles which spies are supposed to bring back to their employers. Some of those men had become abstrusely entangled with the spying departments of other nations and would give an amusing jump if you came from behind and tapped them on the shoulder. A few went a-scouting for the fun of the thing. One or two perhaps really believed that in some mystical way they were preparing the resurrection of a sacred, if somewhat musty, past.

2

We are now going to witness a most weirdly monotonous series of events. The first president of the W.W. to die was the leader of the whole White movement and by far the best man of the lot; and certain dark symptoms attending his sudden illness suggested a poisoner's shadow. The next president, a huge, strong fellow with a voice of thunder and a head like a cannon ball, was kidnapped by persons unknown; and there are reasons to believe that he died from an overdose of chloroform. The third president—but my reel is going too fast. Actually it took seven years to remove the first two—not because this sort of thing cannot be done more briskly, but because there were particular circumstances that necessitated some very precise timing, so as to co-ordinate one's steady ascent with the spacing of sudden vacancies. Let us explain.

Golubkov was not only a very versatile spy (a triple agent to be exact); he was also an exceedingly ambitious little fellow. Why the vision of presiding over an organization that was but a sunset behind a cemetery happened to be so dear to him is a conundrum only for those who have no hobbies or passions. He wanted it very badly—that is all. What is less intelligible is the faith he had in being able to safeguard his puny existence in the crush between the formidable parties whose dangerous money and dangerous help he received. I want all your attention now, for it would be a pity to miss the subtleties of the situation.

The Soviets could not be much disturbed by the highly improbable prospect of a phantom White Army ever being able to resume war operations against their consolidated bulk; but they could be very much irritated by the fact that scraps of information about forts and factories, gathered by elusive W.W. meddlers, were automatically falling into grateful German hands. The Germans were little interested in the recondite color variations of *émigré* politics, but what did annoy them was the blunt patriotism of a W.W. president every now and then obstructing on ethical grounds the smooth flow of friendly collaboration.

Thus, General Golubkov was a godsend. The Soviets firmly expected that under his rule all W.W. spies would be well known to them—and shrewdly supplied with false information for eager German consumption. The Germans were equally sure that through him they would be guaranteed a good cropping of their own absolutely trustworthy agents distributed among the usual W.W. ones. Neither side had any illusions concerning Golubkov's loyalty, but each assumed that it would turn to its own profit the fluctuations of double-crossing. The dreams of simple Russian folk, hard-working families in remote parts of the Russian diaspora, plying their humble but honest trades, as they would in Saratov or Tver, bearing fragile children and naïvely believing that the W.W. was a kind of King Arthur's Round Table that stood for all that had been, and would be, sweet and decent and strong in fairy tale Russia—these dreams may well strike the film pruners as an excrescence upon the main theme.

When the W.W. was founded, General Golubkov's candidacy (purely theoretical, of course, for nobody expected the leader to die) was very far down the list—not because his legendary gallantry was insufficiently appreciated by his fellow officers, but because he happened to be the youngest general in the army. Toward the time of the next president's election Golubkov had already disclosed such tremendous capacities as an organizer that he felt he could safely cross out quite a few intermediate names in the list, incidentally sparing the lives of their bearers. After the second general had been removed, many of the W.W. members were convinced that General Fedchenko, the next candidate, would surrender in favor of the younger and more efficient man the rights that his age, reputation, and academic distinction entitled him to enjoy. The old gentleman, however, though doubtful of the enjoyment, thought it cowardly to avoid a job that had cost two men their lives. So Golubkov set his teeth and started to dig again.

Physically he lacked attraction. There was nothing of your popular Russian general about him, nothing of that good, burly, popeyed, thick-necked sort. He was lean, frail, with sharp features, a clipped mustache, and the kind of haircut that is called by Russians "hedgehog": short, wiry, upright, and compact. There was a thin silver bracelet round his hairy wrist, and he offered you neat homemade Russian cigarettes or English prune-flavored "Kapstens," as he pronounced it, snugly arranged in an old roomy cigarette case of black leather that had accompanied him through the presumable smoke of numberless battles. He was extremely polite and extremely inconspicuous.

Whenever the Slavska "received," which she would do at the homes of her various Maecenases (a Baltic baron of sorts, a Dr. Bachrach whose first wife had been a famous Carmen, or a Russian merchant of the old school who, in inflation-mad Berlin, was having a wonderful time buying up blocks of houses for ten pounds sterling apiece), her silent husband would unobtrusively thread his way among the visitors, bringing you a sausage-and-cucumber sandwich or a tiny frosty-pale glass of vodka; and while the Slavska sang (on those informal occasions she used to sing seated with her fist at her cheek and her elbow cupped in the palm of her other hand) he would stand apart, leaning against something, or would tiptoe toward a distant ash tray which he would gently place on the fat arm of your chair.

I consider that, artistically, he overstressed his effacement, unwittingly introducing a hired-lackey note—which now seems singularly appropriate; but he of course was trying to base his existence upon the principle of contrast and would get a marvelous thrill from exactly knowing by certain sweet signs—a bent head, a rolling eye—that So-and-so at the far end of the room was drawing a newcomer's attention to the fascinating fact that such a dim, modest man was the hero of incredible exploits in a legendary war (taking towns singlehanded and that sort of thing).

3

German film companies, which kept sprouting like poisonous mushrooms in those days (just before the child of light learned to talk), found cheap labor in hiring those among the Russian *émigrés* whose only hope and profession was their past—that is, a set of totally unreal people—to represent "real" audiences in pictures. The dovetailing of one phantasm into another produced upon a sensitive person the impression of living in a Hall of Mirrors, or rather a prison of mirrors, and not even knowing which was the glass and which was yourself.

Indeed, when I recall the halls where the Slavska sang, both in Berlin and in Paris, and the type of people one saw there, I feel as if I were Technicoloring and sonorizing some very ancient motion picture where life had been a gray vibration and funerals a scamper, and where only the sea had been tinted (a sickly blue), while some hand machine imitated off stage the hiss of the asynchronous surf. A certain shady character, the terror of relief organizations, a bald-headed man with mad eyes, slowly floats across my field of vision with his legs bent in a sitting position, like an elderly fetus, and then miraculously fits into a back-row seat. Our friend the Count is also here, complete with high collar and dingy spats. A venerable but worldly priest, with his cross gently heaving on his ample chest, sits in the front row and looks straight ahead.

The items of these Right Wing festivals that the Slavska's name evokes in my mind were of the same unreal nature as was her audience. A variety artist with a fake Slav name, one of those guitar virtuosos that come as a cheap first in music hall programs, would be most welcome here; and the flashy ornaments on his glass-paneled instrument, and his sky-blue silk pants, would go well with the rest of the show. Then some bearded old rascal in a shabby cutaway coat, former member of the Holy Russ First, would take the chair and vividly describe what the Israel-sons and the Phreema-sons (two secret Semitic tribes) were doing to the Russian people.

And now, ladies and gentlemen, we have the great pleas-ure and honor— There she would stand against a dreadful background of palms and national flags, and moisten her rich painted lips with her pale tongue, and leisurely clasp her kid-gloved hands on her corseted stomach, while her constant accompanist, marble-faced Joseph Levinsky, who had followed her, in the shadow of her song, to the Tsar's private concert hall and to Comrade Lunacharsky's salon, and to nondescript places in Constantinople, produced his brief introductory series of stepping-stone notes.

Sometimes, if the house was of the right sort, she would sing the national anthem before launching upon her limited but ever welcome repertoire. Inevitably there would be that lugubrious "Old Road to Kaluga" (with a thunderstruck pine tree at the forty-ninth verst), and the one that begins, in the German translation printed beneath the Russian text, *"Du bist im Schnee begraben, mein Russland,"* and the ancient folklore ballad (written by a private person in the eighties) about the robber chieftain and his lovely Persian Princess, whom he threw into the Volga when his crew accused him of going soft.

Her artistic taste was nowhere, her technique haphazard, her general style atrocious; but the kind of people for whom music and sentiment are one, or who like songs to be mediums for the spirits of circumstances under which they had been first apprehended in an individual past, gratefully found in the tremendous sonorities of her voice both a nostalgic solace and a patriotic kick. She was considered especially effective when a strain of wild recklessness rang through her song. Had this abandon been less blatantly shammed it might still have saved her from utter vulgarity. The small, hard thing that was her soul stuck out of her song, and the most her temperament could attain was but an eddy, not a free torrent. When nowadays in some Russian household the Gramophone is put on, and I hear her canned contralto, it is with something of a shudder that I recall the meretricious imitation she gave of reaching her vocal climax, the anatomy of her mouth fully displayed in a last passionate cry, her blue-black hair beautifully waved, her crossed hands pressed to the beribboned medal on her bosom as she acknowledged the orgy of applause, her broad dusky body rigid even when she bowed, crammed as it was into strong silver satin which made her look like a matron of snow or a mermaid of honor.

4

You will see her next (if the censor does not find what follows offensive to piety) kneeling in the honey-colored haze of a crowded Russian church, lustily sobbing side by side with the wife or widow (she knew exactly which) of the general whose kidnapping had been so nicely arranged by her husband and so deftly performed by those big, efficient, anonymous men that the boss had sent down to Paris.

You will see her also on another day, two or three years later, while she is singing in a certain *appartement*, Rue George Sand, surrounded by admiring friends—and look, her eyes narrow slightly, her singing smile fades, as her husband, who had been detained by the final details of the business in hand, now quietly slips in and with a soft gesture rebukes a grizzled colonel's attempt to offer him his own seat; and through the unconscious flow of a song delivered for the ten-thousandth time she peers at him (she is slightly nearsighted like Anna Karenin) trying to discern some definite sign, and then, as she drowns and his painted boats sail away, and the last telltale circular ripple on the Volga River, Samara County, dissolves into dull eternity (for this is the very last song that she ever will sing), her husband comes up to her and says in a voice that no clapping of human hands can muffle: "Masha, the tree will be felled tomorrow!"

That bit about the tree was the only dramatic treat that Golubkov allowed himself during his dove-gray career. We shall condone the outburst if we remember that this was the ultimate General blocking his way and that next day's event would automatically bring on his own election. There had been lately some mild jesting among their friends (Russian humor being a wee bird satisfied with a crumb) about the amusing little quarrel that those two big children were having, she petulantly demanding the removal of the huge old poplar that darkened her studio window at their suburban summer house, and he contending that the sturdy old fellow was her greenest admirer (sidesplitting, this) and so ought to be spared. Note too the good-natured roguishness of the fat lady in the ermine cape as she taunts the gallant General for giving in so soon, and the Slavska's radiant smile and outstretched jelly-cold arms.

Next day, late in the afternoon, General Golubkov escorted his wife to her dressmaker, sat there for a while reading the *Paris-Soir,* and then was sent back to fetch one of the dresses she wanted loosened and had forgotten to bring. At suitable intervals she gave a passable imitation of telephoning home and volubly directing his search. The dressmaker, an Armenian lady, and a seamstress, little Princess Tumanov, were much entertained in the adjacent room by the variety of her rustic oaths (which helped her not to dry up in a part that her imagination alone could not improvise). This threadbare alibi was not intended for the patching up of past tenses in case anything went wrong —for nothing could go wrong; it was merely meant to provide a man whom none would ever dream of suspecting with a routine account of his movements when people would want to know who had seen General Fedchenko last. After enough imaginary wardrobes had been ransacked Golubkov was seen to return with the dress (which long ago, of course, had been placed in the car). He went on reading his paper while his wife kept trying things on.

5

The thirty-five minutes or so during which he was gone proved quite a comfortable margin. About the time she started fooling with that dead telephone, he had already picked up the General at an unfrequented corner and was driving him to an imaginary appointment the circumstances of which had been so framed in advance as to make its secrecy natural and its attendance a duty. A few minutes later he pulled up and they both got out. "This is not the right street," said General Fedchenko. "No," said General Golubkov, "but it is a convenient one to park my car on. I should not like to leave it right in front of the café. We shall take a short cut through that lane. It is only two minutes' walk." "Good, let us walk," said the old man and cleared his throat.

In that particular quarter of Paris the streets are called after various philosophers, and the lane they were following had been named by some well-read city father Rue Pierre Labime. It gently steered you past a dark church and some scaffolding into a vague region of shuttered private houses standing somewhat aloof within their own grounds behind iron railings on which moribund maple leaves would pause in their flight between bare branch and wet pavement. Along the left side of that lane there was a long wall with crossword puzzles of brick showing here and there through its rough grayness; and in that wall there was at one spot a little green door.

As they approached it, General Golubkov produced his battle-scarred cigarette case and presently stopped to light up. General Fedchenko, a courteous non-smoker, stopped too. There was a gusty wind ruffling the dusk, and the first match went out. "I still think—" said General Fedchenko in reference to some petty business they had been discussing lately, "I still think," he said (to say something as he stood near that little green door), "that if Father Fedor insists on paying for all those lodgings out of his own funds, the least we can do is to supply the fuel." The second match went out too. The back of a passer-by hazily receding in the distance at last disappeared. General Golubkov cursed the wind at the top of his voice, and as this was the all-clear signal the green door opened and three pairs of hands with incredible speed and skill whisked the old man out of sight. The door slammed. General Golubkov lighted his cigarette and briskly walked back the way he had come.

The old man was never seen again. The quiet foreigners who had rented a certain quiet house for one quiet month had been innocent Dutchmen or Danes. It was but an optical trick. There is no green door, but only a gray one, which no human strength can burst open. I have vainly searched through admirable encyclopedias: there is no philosopher called Pierre Labime.

But I have seen the toad in her eyes. We have a saying in Russian: *vsevo dvoe i est; smert' da sovest'*—which may be rendered thus: "There are only two things that really exist —one's death and one's conscience." The lovely thing about humanity is that at times one may be unaware of doing right, but one is always aware of doing wrong. A very horrible criminal, whose wife had been even a worse one, once told me in the days when I was a priest that what had troubled him all through was the inner shame of being stopped by a still deeper shame from discussing with her the puzzle: whether perhaps in her heart of hearts she despised him or whether she secretly wondered if perhaps in his heart of hearts he despised her. And that is why I know perfectly well the kind of face General Golubkov and his wife had when the two were at last alone.

6

Not for very long, however. About 10 P.M. General L., the W.W. Secretary, was informed by General R. that Mrs. Fedchenko was extremely worried by her husband's unaccountable absence. Only then did General L. remember that about lunch time the President had told him in a rather casual way (but that was the old gentleman's manner) that he had some business in town in the late afternoon and that if he was not back by 8 P.M. would General L. please read a note left in the middle drawer of the President's desk. The two generals now rushed to the office, stopped short, rushed back for the keys General L. had forgotten, rushed again, and finally found the note. It read: "An odd feeling obsesses me of which later I may be ashamed. I have an appointment at 5:30 P.M. in a café 45 Rue Descartes. I am to meet an informer from the other side. I suspect a trap. The whole thing has been arranged by General Golubkov, who is taking me there in his car."

We shall skip what General L. said and what General R. replied—but apparently they were slow thinkers and proceeded to lose some more time in a muddled telephone talk with an indignant café owner. It was almost midnight when the Slavska, clad in a flowery dressing gown and trying to look very sleepy, let them in. She was unwilling to disturb her husband, who, she said, was already asleep. She wanted to know what it was all about and had perhaps something happened to General Fedchenko. "He has vanished," said honest General L. The Slavska said, "Akh!" and crashed in a dead swoon, almost wrecking the parlor in the process. The stage had not lost quite so much as most of her admirers thought.

Somehow or other the two generals managed not to impart to General Golubkov anything about the little note, so that when he accompanied them to the W.W. headquarters he was under the impression that they really wanted to discuss with him whether to ring up the police at once or first go for advice to eighty-eight-year-old Admiral Gromoboyev, who for some obscure reason was considered the Solomon of the W.W.

"What does this mean?" said General L. handing the fatal note to Golubkov. "Peruse it, please."

Golubkov perused—and knew at once that all was lost. We shall not bend over the abyss of his feelings. He handed the note back with a shrug of his thin shoulders.

"If this has been really written by the General," he said, "and I must admit it looks very similar to his hand, then all I can say is that somebody has been impersonating me. However, I have grounds to believe that Admiral Gromoboyev will be able to exonerate me. I suggest we go there at once."

"Yes," said General L., "we had better go now, although it is very late."

General Golubkov swished himself into his raincoat and went out first. General R. helped General L. to retrieve his muffler. It had half slipped down from one of those vestibule chairs which are doomed to accommodate things, not people. General L. sighed and put on his old felt hat, using both hands for this gentle action. He moved to the door. "One moment, General," said General R. in a low voice. "I want to ask you something. As one officer to another, are you absolutely sure that . . . well, that General Golubkov is speaking the truth?"

"That's what we shall find out," answered General L., who was one of those people who believe that so long as a sentence is a sentence it is bound to mean something.

They delicately touched each other's elbows in the doorway. Finally the slightly older man accepted the privilege and made a jaunty exit. Then they both paused on the landing, for the staircase struck them as being very still. "General!" cried General L. in a downward direction. Then they looked at each other. Then hurriedly, clumsily, they stomped down the ugly steps, and emerged, and stopped under a black drizzle, and looked this way and that, and then at each other again.

She was arrested early on the following morning. Never once during the inquest did she depart from her attitude of grief-stricken innocence. The French police displayed a queer listlessness in dealing with possible clews, as if it

assumed that the disappearance of Russian generals was a
kind of curious local custom, an Oriental phenomenon, a
dissolving process which perhaps ought not to occur but
which could not be prevented. One had, however, the impression that the *Sûreté* knew more about the workings of
that vanishing trick than diplomatic wisdom found fit to
discuss. Newspapers abroad treated the whole matter in
a good-natured but bantering and slightly bored manner.
On the whole, "L'affaire Slavska" did not make good head-
lines—Russian *émigrés* were decidedly out of focus. By an
amusing coincidence both a German press agency and a
Soviet one laconically stated that a pair of White Russian
generals in Paris had absconded with the White Army
funds.

<h2 style="text-align:center">7</h2>

The trial was strangely inconclusive and muddled, witnesses did not shine, and the final conviction of the Slavska
on a charge of kidnapping was debatable on legal grounds.
Irrelevant trifles kept obscuring the main issue. The wrong
people remembered the right things and vice versa. There
was a bill signed by a certain Gaston Coulot, farmer, "*pour
un arbre abattu.*" General L. and General R. had a dreadful time at the hands of a sadistic barrister. A Parisian
clochard, one of those colorful ripe-nosed unshaven beings
(an easy part, that) who keep all their earthly belongings
in their voluminous pockets and wrap their feet in layers
of bursting newspapers when the last sock is gone and are
seen comfortably seated, with widespread legs and a bottle
of wine against the crumbling wall of some building that
has never been completed, gave a lurid account of having
observed from a certain vantage point an old man being

roughly handled. Two Russian women, one of whom had been treated some time before for acute hysteria, said they saw on the day of the crime General Golubkov and General Fedchenko driving in the former's car. A Russian violinist while sitting in the diner of a German train—but it is useless to retell all those lame rumors.

We get a few last glimpses of the Slavska in prison. Meekly knitting in a corner. Writing to Mrs. Fedchenko tear-stained letters in which she said that they were sisters now, because both their husbands had been captured by the Bolsheviks. Begging to be allowed the use of a lipstick. Sobbing and praying in the arms of a pale young Russian nun who had come to tell her of a vision she had had which disclosed the innocence of General Golubkov. Clamoring for the New Testament which the police were keeping— keeping mainly from the experts who had so nicely begun deciphering certain notes scribbled in the margin of St. John's Gospel. Some time after the outbreak of World War II, she developed an obscure internal trouble and when, one summer morning, three German officers arrived at the prison hospital and desired to see her, at once, they were told she was dead—which possibly was the truth.

Boston, 1943.

The Aurelian

1

Luring aside one of the trolley-car numbers, the street started at the corner of a crowded avenue. For a long time it crept on in obscurity, with no shopwindows or any such joys. Then came a small square (four benches, a bed of pansies) round which the trolley steered with rasping disapproval. Here the street changed its name, and a new life began. Along the right side, shops appeared: a fruiterer's, with vivid pyramids of oranges; a tobacconist's, with the picture of a voluptuous Turk; a delicatessen, with fat brown and gray coils of sausages; and then, all of a sudden, a butterfly store. At night, and especially when it was damp, with the asphalt shining like the back of a seal, passers-by would stop for a second before that symbol of fair weather. The insects on exhibit were huge and gorgeous. People would say to themselves, "What colors—amazing!" and plod on through the drizzle. Eyed wings wide-open in wonder, shimmering blue satin, black magic—these lingered for a while floating in one's vision, until one boarded the trolley or bought a newspaper. And, just because they were together with the butterflies, a few other objects would remain in one's memory: a globe, pencils, and a monkey's skull on a pile of copybooks.

As the street blinked and ran on, there followed again a succession of ordinary shops—soap, coal, bread—with another pause at the corner where there was a small bar. The bartender, a dashing fellow in a starched collar and green sweater, was deft at shaving off with one stroke the foam topping the glass under the beer tap; he also had a well-earned reputation as a wit. Every night, at a round table by the window, the fruiterer, the baker, an unemployed man, and the bartender's first cousin played cards with great gusto. As the winner of the current stake immediately ordered four drinks, none of the players could ever get rich.

On Saturdays, at an adjacent table, there would sit a flabby elderly man with a florid face, lank hair, and a grayish mustache, carelessly clipped. When he appeared, the players greeted him noisily without looking up from their cards. He invariably ordered rum, filled his pipe, and gazed at the game with pink-rimmed watery eyes. The left eyelid drooped slightly.

Occasionally someone turned to him, and asked how his shop was doing; he would be slow to answer, and often did not answer at all. If the bartender's daughter, a pretty freckled girl in a polka-dotted frock, happened to pass close enough, he had a go at her elusive hip, and, whether the slap succeeded or not, his gloomy expression never changed, although the veins on his temple grew purple. Mine host very humorously called him "Herr Professor."

"Well, how is the Herr Professor tonight?" he would ask, coming over to him, and the man would ponder for some time in silence and then, with a wet underlip pushing out from under the pipe like that of a feeding elephant, he would answer something neither funny nor polite. The bartender would counter briskly, which made the players at the next table, though seemingly absorbed in their cards, rock with ugly glee.

The man wore a roomy gray suit with great exaggeration of the vest motif, and when the cuckoo popped out of the clock he ponderously extracted a thick silver watch and gazed at it askance, holding it in the palm of his hand and squinting because of the smoke. Punctually at eleven he knocked out his pipe, paid for his rum, and, after extending a flaccid hand to anyone who might choose to shake it, silently left.

He walked awkwardly, with a slight limp. His legs seemed too thin for his body. Just before the window of his shop he turned into a passage, where there was a door on the right with a brass plate: PAUL PILGRAM. This door led into his tiny dingy apartment, which could also be reached by an inner corridor at the back of the shop. Eleanor was usually asleep when he came home on those festive nights. Half a dozen faded photographs of the same clumsy ship, taken from different angles, and of a palm tree that looked as bleak as if it were growing on Helgoland hung in black frames above the double bed. Muttering to himself, Pilgram limped away into bulbless darkness with a lighted candle, came back with his suspenders dangling, and kept muttering while sitting on the edge of the bed and slowly, painfully, taking off his shoes. His wife, half-waking, moaned into her pillow and offered to help him; and then with a threatening rumble in his voice, he would tell her to keep quiet, and repeated that guttural *"Ruhe!"* several times, more and more fiercely.

After the stroke which had almost killed him some time ago (like a mountain falling upon him from behind just as he had bent towards his shoestrings), he now undressed reluctantly, growling until he got safely into bed, and then growling again if the faucet happened to drip in the adjoining kitchen. Eleanor would roll out of bed and totter into the kitchen and totter back with a dazed sigh, her small face wax-pale and shiny, and the plastered corns on her feet showing from under her dismally long nightgown. They had married in 1905, almost a quarter of a century before, and were childless because Pilgram had always thought that children would be merely a hindrance to the realization of what had been in his youth a delightfully exciting plan but had now gradually become a dark, passionate obsession.

He slept on his back with an old-fashioned nightcap coming down on his forehead; it was to all appearances the solid and sonorous sleep that might be expected in an elderly German shopkeeper, and one could readily suppose that his quilted torpor was entirely devoid of visions; but actually this churlish, heavy man, who fed mainly on *Erbswurst* and boiled potatoes, placidly believing in his newspaper and quite ignorant of the world (insofar as his secret passion was not involved), dreamed of things that would have seemed utterly unintelligible to his wife or his neighbors; for Pilgram belonged, or rather was meant to belong (something—the place, the time, the man—had been ill-chosen), to a special breed of dreamers, such dreamers as used to be called in the old days "Aurelians"—perhaps on account of those chrysalids, those "jewels of nature," which they loved to find hanging on fences above the dusty nettles of country lanes.

On Sundays he drank his morning coffee in several sloppy sessions, and then went out for a walk with his wife, a slow silent stroll which Eleanor looked forward to all week. On workdays he opened his shop as early as possible because of the children who passed by on their way to school; for lately he had been keeping school supplies in addition to his basic stock. Some small boy, swinging his satchel and chewing a sandwich, would slouch past the tobacconist's (where a certain brand of cigarettes offered airplane pictures), past the delicatessen (which rebuked one for having eaten that sandwich long before lunchtime), and then, remembering he wanted an eraser, would enter the next shop. Pilgram would mumble something, sticking out his lower lip from under the stem of his pipe, and, after a listless search, would plump down an open carton on the counter. The boy would feel and squeeze the virgin-pale India rubber, would not find the sort he favored, and would leave without even noticing the principal wares in the store.

"These modern children!" Pilgram would think with disgust and he recalled his own boyhood. His father—a sailor, a rover, a bit of a rogue—married late in life a sallow-skinned, light-eyed Dutch girl whom he brought from Java to Berlin, and opened a shop of exotic curios. Pilgram could not remember now when, exactly, butterflies had begun to oust the stuffed birds of paradise, the stale talismans, the fans with dragons, and the like; but as a boy he already feverishly swapped specimens with collectors, and after his parents died butterflies reigned supreme in the dim little shop. Up to 1914 there were enough amateurs and professionals about to keep things going in a mild, very mild, way; later on, however, it became necessary to make

99

concessions, a display case with the biography of the silk-worm furnishing a transition to school supplies, just as in the old days pictures ignominiously composed of sparkling wings had probably been a first step towards lepidopterology.

Now the window contained, apart from penholders, mainly showy insects, popular stars among butterflies, some of them set on plaster and framed—intended merely for ornamenting the home. In the shop itself, permeated with the pungent odor of a disinfectant, the real, the precious collections were kept. The whole place was littered with various cases, cartons, cigar boxes. Tall cabinets contained numerous glass-lidded drawers filled with ordered series of perfect specimens impeccably spread and labeled. A dusty old shield or something (last remnant of the original wares) stood in a dark corner. Now and then live stock would appear: loaded brown pupae with a symmetrical confluence of delicate lines and grooves on the thorax, showing how the rudimentary wings, feet, antennae, and proboscis were packed. If one touched such a pupa as it lay on its bed of moss, the tapering end of the segmented abdomen would start jerking this way and that like the swathed limbs of a baby. The pupae cost a reichsmark apiece and in due time yielded a limp bedraggled, miraculously expanding moth. And sometimes other creatures would be temporarily on sale: just then there happened to be a dozen lizards, natives of Majorca, cold, black, blue-bellied things, which Pilgram fed on meal worms for the main course and grapes for dessert.

2

He had spent all his life in Berlin and its suburbs; had

never traveled farther than Peacock Island on a neighboring lake. He was a first-class entomologist. Dr. Rebel, of Vienna, had named a certain rare moth *Agrotis pilgrami;* and Pilgram himself had published several descriptions. His boxes contained most of the countries of the world, but all he had ever seen of it was the dull sand-and-pine scenery of an occasional Sunday trip; and he would be reminded of captures that had seemed to him so miraculous in his boyhood as he melancholically gazed at the familiar fauna about him, limited by a familiar landscape, to which it corresponded as hopelessly as he to his street. From a roadside shrub he would pick up a large turquoise-green caterpillar with a china-blue horn on the last ring; there it lay quite stiff on the palm of his hand, and presently, with a sigh, he would put it back on its twig as if it were some dead trinket.

Although once or twice he had had the chance to switch to a more profitable business—selling cloth, for instance, instead of moths—he stubbornly held on to his shop as the symbolic link between his dreary existence and the phantom of perfect happiness. What he craved for, with a fierce, almost morbid intensity, was *himself* to net the rarest butterflies of distant countries, to see them in flight with his own eyes, to stand waist-deep in lush grass and feel the follow-through of the swishing net and then the furious throbbing of wings through a clutched fold of the gauze.

Every year it seemed to him stranger that the year before he had not managed somehow to lay aside enough money for at least a fortnight's collecting trip abroad, but he had never been thrifty, business had always been slack, there was always a gap somewhere, and, even if luck did come his way now and then, something was sure to go wrong at the last moment. He had married counting heavily on a share in his father-in-law's business, but a month later the man had died, leaving nothing but debts. Just before World War I an unexpected deal brought a journey to Algeria so near that he even acquired a sun helmet. When all travel stopped, he still consoled himself with the hope that he might be sent to some exciting place as a soldier; but he was clumsy, sickly, not very young, and thus saw neither active service nor exotic Lepidoptera. Then, after the war, when he had managed again to save a little money (for a week in Zermatt, this time), the inflation suddenly turned his meager hoard into something less than the price of a trolley car ticket.

After that he gave up trying. He grew more and more depressed as his passion grew stronger. When some entomological acquaintance happened to drop in, Pilgram was only annoyed. "That fellow," he would think, "may be as learned as the late Dr. Staudinger, but he has no more imagination than a stamp collector." The glass-lidded trays over which both were bending gradually took up the whole counter, and the pipe in Pilgram's sucking lips kept emitting a wistful squeak. Pensively he gazed at the serried rows of delicate insects, all alike to you or me, and now and then he tapped on the glass with a stubby forefinger, stressing some special rarity. "That's a curiously dark aberration," the learned visitor might say. "Eisner got one like that at an auction in London, but it was not so dark, and it cost him £14." Painfully sniffling with his extinguished pipe, Pilgram would raise the box to the light, which made the shadows of the butterflies slip from beneath them across the papered bottom; then he would put it down again, and, working in his nails under the tight edges of the lid, would shake it loose with a jerk and smoothly remove it. "And Eisner's female was not so fresh," the visitor would add, and some eavesdroppers coming in for a copybook or a postage stamp might well wonder what on earth these two were talking about.

Grunting, Pilgram plucked at the gilded head of the black pin upon which the silky little creature was crucified, and took the specimen out of the box. Turning it this way and that, he peered at the label pinned under the body. "Yes—Tatsienlu, East Tibet," he read. "Taken by the native collectors of Father Dejean" (which sounded almost like "Prester John")—and he would stick the butterfly back again, right into the same pinhole. His motions seemed casual, even careless, but this was the unerring nonchalance of the specialist: the pin, with the precious insect, and Pilgram's fat fingers were the correlated parts of one and the same flawless machine. It might happen, however, that some open box, having been brushed by the elbow of the visitor, would stealthily begin to slide off the counter—to be stopped just in the nick of time by Pilgram, who would then calmly go on lighting his pipe; only much later, when busy elsewhere, he would suddenly produce a moan of retrospective anguish.

But not only averted crashes made him moan. Father Dejean, stout-hearted missionary climbing among the rhododendrons and snows, how enviable was thy lot! And Pilgram would stare at his boxes and puff and brood and reflect that he need not go so far: that there were thousands of hunting grounds all over Europe. Out of localities cited in entomological works he had built up a special world of his own, to which his science was a most detailed guidebook. In that world there were no casinos, no old churches, nothing that might attract a normal tourist. Digne in southern France, Ragusa in Dalmatia, Sarepta on the Volga, Abisko in Lapland—those were the famous sites dear to butterfly collectors, and this is where they had poked about, on and off, since the fifties of the last century (always greatly perplexing the local inhabitants). And as clearly as if it were a reminiscence Pilgram saw himself troubling the sleep of a little hotel by stamping and jumping about a room through the wide-open window of which, out of the black generous night, a whitish moth had dashed in and, in an audible bob dance, was kissing its shadow all over the ceiling.

In these impossible dreams of his he visited the Islands of the Blessed, where in the hot ravines that cut the lower slopes of the chestnut- and laurel-clad mountains there occurs a weird local race of the cabbage white; and also that other island, those railway banks near Vizzavona and the pine woods farther up, which are the haunts of the squat and dusky Corsican swallowtail. He visited the far North, the arctic bogs that produced such delicate downy butterflies. He knew the high Alpine pastures, with those flat stones lying here and there among the slippery matted grass; for there is no greater delight than to lift such a stone and find beneath it a plump sleepy moth of a still undescribed species. He saw glazed Apollo butterflies, ocellated with red, float in the mountain draft across the mule track that ran between a steep cliff and an abyss of wild white waters. In Italian gardens in the summer dusk, the gravel crunched invitingly underfoot, and Pilgram gazed through the growing darkness at clusters of blossoms in front of which suddenly there appeared an oleander hawk, which passed from flower to flower, humming intently and stopping at the corolla, its wings vibrating so rapidly that nothing but a ghostly nimbus was visible about its streamlined body. And best of all, perhaps, were the white heathered hills near Madrid, the valleys of Andalusia, fertile and wooded Albarracin, whither a little bus driven by the forest guard's brother groaned up a twisted road.

He had more difficulty in imagining the tropics, but experienced still keener pangs when he did, for never would he catch the loftily flapping Brazilian morphos, so ample and radiant that they cast an azure reflection upon one's hand, never come upon those crowds of African butterflies closely stuck like innumerable fancy flags into the rich black mud and rising in a colored cloud when his shadow approached—a long, very long, shadow.

3

"*Ja, ja, ja,*" he would mutter, nodding his heavy head, and holding the case before him as if it were a beloved portrait. The bell over the door would tinkle, his wife would come in with a wet umbrella and a shopping bag, and slowly he would turn his back to her as he inserted the case into the cabinet. So it went on, that obsession and that despair and that nightmarish impossibility to swindle destiny, until a certain first of April, of all dates. For more than a year he had had in his keeping a cabinet devoted solely to the genus of those small clear-winged moths that mimic wasps or mosquitoes. The widow of a great authority on that particular group had given Pilgram her husband's collection to sell on commission. He hastened to tell the silly woman that he would not be able to get more than 75 marks for it, although he knew very well that, according to catalogue prices, it was worth fifty times more, so that the amateur to whom he would sell the lot for, say, a thousand marks would consider it a good bargain. The amateur, however, did not appear, though Pilgram had written to all the wealthiest collectors. So he had locked up the cabinet, and stopped thinking about it.

That April morning a sunburned, bespectacled man in an old mackintosh and without any hat on his brown bald head sauntered in, and asked for some carbon paper. Pilgram slipped the small coins paid for the sticky violet stuff he so hated to handle into the slit of a small clay money pot, and, sucking on his pipe, fixed his stare into space. The man cast a rapid glance round the shop, and remarked upon the extravagant brilliancy of an iridescent green insect with many tails. Pilgram mumbled something about Madagascar. "And that—that's not a butterfly, is it?" said the man, indicating another specimen. Pilgram slowly replied that he had a whole collection of that special kind. "*Ach, was!*" said the man. Pilgram scratched his bristly chin, and limped into a recess of the shop. He pulled out a glass-topped tray, and laid it on the counter. The man pored over those tiny vitreous creatures with bright orange feet and belted bodies. Pilgram pointed with the stem of his pipe to one of the rows, and simultaneously the man exclaimed: "Good God—*uralensis!*" and that ejaculation gave him away. Pilgram heaped case after case on the counter as it dawned upon him that the visitor knew perfectly well of the existence of this collection, had come for its sake, was as a matter of fact the rich amateur Sommer, to whom he had written and who had just returned from a trip to Venezuela; and finally, when the question was carelessly put—"Well, and what would the price be?"—Pilgram smiled.

He knew it was madness; he knew he was leaving a helpless Eleanor, debts, unpaid taxes, a store at which only trash was bought; he knew that the 950 marks he might get would permit him to travel for no longer than a few months; and still he accepted it all as a man who felt that tomorrow would bring dreary old age and that the good fortune which now beckoned would never again repeat its invitation.

When finally Sommer said that on the fourth he would give a definite answer, Pilgram decided that the dream of his life was about to break at last from its old crinkly cocoon. He spent several hours examining a map, choosing a route, estimating the time of appearance of this or that species, and suddenly something black and blinding welled before his eyes, and he stumbled about his shop for quite a while before he felt better. The fourth came and Sommer failed to turn up, and, after waiting all day, Pilgram retired to his bedroom and silently lay down. He refused his supper, and for several minutes, with his eyes closed, nagged his wife, thinking she was still standing near; then he heard her sobbing softly in the kitchen, and toyed with the idea of taking an ax and splitting her pale-haired head. Next day he stayed in bed, and Eleanor took his place in the shop and sold a box of water colors. And after still another day, when the whole thing seemed merely delirium, Sommer, a carnation in his buttonhole and his mackintosh on his arm, entered the store. And when he took out a wad, and the banknotes rustled, Pilgram's nose began to bleed violently.

The delivery of the cabinet and a visit to the credulous old woman, to whom he reluctantly gave 50 marks, were his last business in town. The much more expensive visit to the traveling agency already referred to his new existence, where only butterflies mattered. Eleanor, though not familiar with her husband's transactions, looked happy, feeling that he had made a good profit, but fearing to ask how much. That afternoon a neighbor dropped in to remind them that tomorrow was the wedding of his daughter. So next morning Eleanor busied herself with brightening up her silk dress and pressing her husband's best suit. She would go there about five, she thought, and he would follow later, after closing time. When he looked up at her with a puzzled frown and then flatly refused to go, it did not surprise her, for she had long become used to all sorts of disappointments. "There might be champagne," she said, when already standing in the doorway. No answer—only the shuffling of boxes. She looked thoughtfully at the nice clean gloves on her hands, and went out.

Pilgram, having put the more valuable collections in order, looked at his watch and saw it was time to pack: his train left at 8:29. He locked the shop, dragged out of the corridor his father's old checkered suitcase, and packed the hunting implements first: a folding net, killing jars, pill-boxes, a lantern for mothing at night on the sierras, and a few packages of pins. As an afterthought he put in a couple of spreading boards and a cork-bottomed box, though in general he intended to keep his captures in papers, as is usually done when going from place to place. Then he took the suitcase into the bedroom and threw in some thick socks and underwear. He added two or three things that might be sold in an extremity, such as, for instance, a silver tumbler and a bronze medal in a velvet case, which had belonged to his father-in-law.

Again he looked at his watch, and then decided it was time to start for the station. "Eleanor!" he called loudly, getting into his overcoat. As she did not reply, he looked into the kitchen. No, she was not there; and then vaguely he remembered something about a wedding. Hurriedly he got a scrap of paper and scribbled a few words in pencil.

He left the note and the keys in a conspicuous place, and with a chill of excitement, a sinking feeling in the pit of the stomach, verified for the last time whether the money and tickets were in his wallet. "*Also los!*" said Pilgram, and gripped the suitcase.

But, as it was his first journey, he still kept worrying nervously whether there was anything he might have forgotten; then it occurred to him that he had no small change, and he remembered the clay money pot where there might be a few coins. Groaning and knocking the heavy suitcase against corners, he returned to his counter. In the twilight of the strangely still shop, eyed wings stared at him from all sides, and Pilgram perceived something almost appalling in the richness of the huge happiness that was leaning toward him like a mountain. Trying to avoid the knowing looks of those numberless eyes, he drew a deep breath and, catching sight of the hazy money pot, which seemed to hang in mid-air, reached quickly for it. The pot slipped from his moist grasp and broke on the floor with a dizzy spinning of twinkling coins; and Pilgram bent low to pick them up.

4

Night came; a slippery polished moon sped, without the least friction, in between chinchilla clouds, and Eleanor, returning from the wedding supper, and still all atingle from the wine and the juicy jokes, recalled her own wedding day as she leisurely walked home. Somehow all the thoughts now passing through her brain kept turning so as to show their moon-bright, attractive side; she felt almost light-hearted as she entered the gateway and proceeded to open the door, and she caught herself thinking that it was surely a great thing to have an apartment of one's own, stuffy and dark though it might be. Smiling, she turned on the light in her bedroom, and saw at once that all the drawers had been pulled open: she hardly had time to imagine burglars, for there were those keys on the night table and a bit of paper propped against the alarm clock. The note was brief: "Off to Spain. Don't touch anything till I write. Borrow from Sch. or W. Feed the lizards."

The faucet was dripping in the kitchen. Unconsciously she picked up her silver bag where she had dropped it, and kept on sitting on the edge of the bed, quite straight and still, with her hands in her lap as if she were having her photograph taken. After a time someone got up, walked across the room, inspected the bolted window, came back again, while she watched with indifference, not realizing that it was she who was moving. The drops of water plopped in slow succession, and suddenly she felt terrified at being alone in the house. The man whom she had loved for his mute omniscience, stolid coarseness, grim perseverance in work, had stolen away. . . . She felt like howling, running to the police, showing her marriage certificate, insisting, pleading; but still she kept on sitting, her hair slightly ruffled, her hands in white gloves.

Yes, Pilgram had gone far, very far. Most probably he visited Granada and Murcia and Albarracin, and then traveled farther still, to Surinam or Taprobane; and one can hardly doubt that he saw all the glorious bugs he had longed to see—velvety black butterflies soaring over the jungles, and a tiny moth in Tasmania, and that Chinese "skipper" said to smell of crushed roses when alive, and the short-clubbed beauty that a Mr. Baron had just discovered in Mexico. So, in a certain sense, it is quite irrelevant that some time later, upon wandering into the shop, Eleanor saw the checkered suitcase, and then her husband, sprawling on the floor with his back to the counter, among scattered coins, his livid face knocked out of shape by death.

Berlin, 1931.

Cloud, Castle, Lake

One of my representatives—a modest, mild bachelor, very efficient—happened to win a pleasure trip at a charity ball given by Russian refugees. That was in 1936 or 1937. The Berlin summer was in full flood (it was the second week of damp and cold, so that it was a pity to look at everything which had turned green in vain, and only the sparrows kept cheerful); he did not care to go anywhere, but when he tried to sell his ticket at the office of the Bureau of Pleasantrips he was told that to do so he would have to have special permission from the Ministry of Transportation; when he tried them, it turned out that first he would have to draw up a complicated petition at a notary's on stamped paper; and besides, a so-called "certificate of non-absence from the city for the summertime" had to be obtained from the police.

So he sighed a little, and decided to go. He borrowed

an aluminum flask from friends, repaired his soles, bought a belt and a fancy-style flannel shirt—one of those cowardly things which shrink in the first wash. Incidentally, it was too large for that likable little man, his hair always neatly trimmed, his eyes so intelligent and kind. I cannot remember his name at the moment. I think it was Vasili Ivanovich.

He slept badly the night before the departure. And why? Because he had to get up unusually early, and hence took along into his dreams the delicate face of the watch ticking on his night table; but mainly because that very night, for no reason at all, he began to imagine that this trip, thrust upon him by a feminine Fate in a low-cut gown, this trip which he had accepted so reluctantly, would bring him some wonderful, tremulous happiness. This happiness would have something in common with his childhood, and with the excitement aroused in him by Russian lyrical poetry, and with some evening sky line once seen in a dream, and with that lady, another man's wife, whom he had hopelessly loved for seven years—but it would be even fuller and more significant than all that. And besides, he felt that the really good life must be oriented toward something or someone.

The morning was dull, but steam-warm and close, with an inner sun, and it was quite pleasant to rattle in a streetcar to the distant railway station where the gathering place was: several people, alas, were taking part in the excursion. Who would they be, these drowsy beings, drowsy as seem all creatures still unknown to us? By Window No. 6, at 7 A.M., as was indicated in the directions appended to the ticket, he saw them (they were already waiting; he had managed to be late by about three minutes).

A lanky blond young man in Tyrolese garb stood out at once. He was burned the color of a cockscomb, had huge brick-red knees with golden hairs, and his nose looked lacquered. He was the leader furnished by the Bureau, and as soon as the newcomer had joined the group (which consisted of four women and as many men) he led it off toward a train lurking behind other trains, carrying his monstrous knapsack with terrifying ease, and firmly clanking with his hobnailed boots.

Everyone found a place in an empty car, unmistakably third-class, and Vasili Ivanovich, having sat down by himself and put a peppermint into his mouth, opened a little volume of Tyutchev, whom he had long intended to re-read; but he was requested to put the book aside and join the group. An elderly bespectacled post-office clerk, with skull, chin, and upper lip a bristly blue as if he had shaved off some extraordinarily luxuriant and tough growth especially for this trip, immediately announced that he had been to Russia and knew some Russian —for instance, *patzlui*—and, recalling philanderings in Tsaritsyn, winked in such a manner that his fat wife sketched out in the air the outline of a backhand box on the ear. The company was getting noisy. Four employees of the same building firm were tossing each other heavy-weight jokes: a middle-aged man, Schultz; a younger man, Schultz also, and two fidgety young women with big mouths and big rumps. The red-headed, rather burlesque widow in a sport skirt knew something too about Russia (the Riga beaches). There was also a dark young man by the name of Schramm, with lusterless eyes and a vague velvety vileness about his person and manners, who constantly switched the conversation to this or that attractive aspect of the excursion, and who gave the first signal for rapturous appreciation; he was, as it turned out later, a special stimulator from the Bureau of Pleasantrips.

The locomotive, working rapidly with its elbows, hurried through a pine forest, then—with relief—among fields. Only dimly realizing as yet all the absurdity and horror of the situation, and perhaps attempting to persuade himself that everything was very nice, Vasili Ivanovich contrived to enjoy the fleeting gifts of the road. And indeed, how enticing it all is, what charm the world acquires when it is wound up and moving like a merry-go-round! The sun crept toward a corner of the window and suddenly spilled over the yellow bench. The badly pressed shadow of the car sped madly along the grassy bank, where flowers blended into colored streaks. A crossing: a cyclist was waiting, one foot resting on the ground. Trees appeared in groups and singly, revolving coolly and blandly, displaying the latest fashions. The blue dampness of a ravine. A memory of love, disguised as a meadow. Wispy clouds—greyhounds of heaven.

We both, Vasili Ivanovich and I, have always been impressed by the anonymity of all the parts of a landscape, so dangerous for the soul, the impossibility of ever finding out where that path you see leads—and look, what a tempting thicket! It happened that on a distant slope or in a gap in the trees there would appear and, as it were, stop for an instant, like air retained in the lungs, a spot so enchanting—a lawn, a terrace—such perfect expression of tender well-meaning beauty—that it seemed that if one could stop the train and go thither, forever, to you, my love . . . But a thousand beech trunks were already madly leaping by, whirling in a sizzling sun pool, and again the chance for happiness was gone.

At the stations, Vasili Ivanovich would look at the configuration of some entirely insignificant objects—a smear on the platform, a cherry stone, a cigarette butt—and would say to himself that never, never would he remember these three little things here in that particular interrelation, this pattern, which he now could see with such deathless precision; or again, looking at a group of children waiting for a train, he would try with all his might to single out at least one remarkable destiny—in the form of a violin or a crown, a propeller or a lyre—and would gaze until the whole party of village schoolboys appeared as on an old photograph, now reproduced with a little white cross above the face of the last boy on the right: the hero's childhood.

But one could look out of the window only by snatches. All had been given sheet music with verses from the Bureau:

> Stop that worrying and moping,
> Take a knotted stick and rise,
> Come a-tramping in the open
> With the good, the hearty guys!

> Tramp your country's grass and stubble,
> With the good, the hearty guys,
> Kill the hermit and his trouble
> And to hell with doubts and sighs!

> In a paradise of heather
> Where the field mouse screams and dies,
> Let us march and sweat together
> With the steel-and-leather guys!

This was to be sung in chorus: Vasili Ivanovich, who not only could not sing but could not even pronounce German words clearly, took advantage of the drowning roar of mingling voices and merely opened his mouth while swaying slightly, as if he were really singing—but the leader, at a sign from the subtle Schramm, suddenly stopped the general singing and, squinting askance at Vasili Ivanovich, demanded that he sing solo. Vasili Ivanovich cleared his throat, timidly began, and after a minute of solitary torment all joined in; but he did not dare thereafter to drop out.

He had with him his favorite cucumber from the Russian store, a loaf of bread, and three eggs. When evening came, and the low crimson sun entered wholly the soiled seasick car, stunned by its own din, all were invited to hand over their provisions, in order to divide them evenly—this was particularly easy, as all except Vasili Ivanovich had the same things. The cucumber amused everybody, was pronounced inedible, and was thrown out of the window. In view of the insufficiency of his contribution, Vasili Ivanovich got a smaller portion of sausage.

He was made to play cards. They pulled him about, questioned him, verified whether he could show the route of the trip on a map—in a word, all busied themselves with him, at first good-naturedly, then with malevolence, which grew with the approach of night. Both girls were called Greta; the red-headed widow somehow resembled the rooster-leader; Schramm, Schultz, and the other Schultz, the post-office clerk and his wife, all gradually melted together, merged together, forming one collective, wobbly, many-handed being, from which one could not escape. It pressed upon him from all sides. But suddenly at some station all climbed out, and it was already dark, although in the west there still hung a very long, very pink cloud, and farther along the track, with a soul-piercing light, the star of a lamp trembled through the slow smoke of the engine, and crickets chirped in the dark, and from somewhere there came the odor of jasmine and hay, my love.

They spent the night in a tumble-down inn. A mature bedbug is awful, but there is a certain grace in the motions of silky silverfish. The post-office clerk was separated from his wife, who was put with the widow; he was given to Vasili Ivanovich for the night. The two beds took up the whole room. Quilt on top, chamber pot below. The clerk said that somehow he did not feel sleepy, and began to talk of his Russian adventures, rather more circumstantially than in the train. He was a great bully of a man, thorough and obstinate, clad in long cotton drawers, with mother-of-pearl claws on his dirty toes, and bear's fur between fat breasts. A moth dashed about the ceiling, hobnobbing with its shadow. "In Tsaritsyn," the clerk was saying, "there are now three schools, a German, a Czech, and a Chinese one. At any rate, that is what my brother-in-law says; he went there to build tractors."

Next day, from early morning to five o'clock in the afternoon, they raised dust along a highway, which undulated from hill to hill; then they took a green road through a dense fir wood. Vasili Ivanovich, as the least burdened, was given an enormous round loaf of bread to carry under his arm. How I hate you, our daily! But still his precious, experienced eyes noted what was necessary. Against the background of fir-tree gloom a dry needle was hanging vertically on an invisible thread.

Again they piled into a train, and again the small partitionless car was empty. The other Schultz began to teach Vasili Ivanovich how to play the mandolin. There was much laughter. When they got tired of that, they thought up a capital game, which was supervised by Schramm. It consisted of the following: the women would lie down on the benches they chose, under which the men were already hidden, and when from under one of the benches there would emerge a ruddy face with ears, or a big outspread hand, with a skirt-lifting curve of the fingers (which would provoke much squealing), then it would be revealed who

119

was paired off with whom. Three times Vasili Ivanovich lay down in filthy darkness, and three times it turned out that there was no one on the bench when he crawled out from under. He was acknowledged the loser and was forced to eat a cigarette butt.

They spent the night on straw mattresses in a barn, and early in the morning set out again on foot. Firs, ravines, foamy streams. From the heat, from the songs which one had constantly to bawl, Vasili Ivanovich became so exhausted that during the midday halt he fell asleep at once, and awoke only when they began to slap at imaginary horseflies on him. But after another hour of marching, that very happiness of which he had once half dreamt was suddenly discovered.

It was a pure, blue lake, with an unusual expression of its water. In the middle, a large cloud was reflected in its entirety. On the other side, on a hill thickly covered with verdure (and the darker the verdure, the more poetic it is), towered, arising from dactyl to dactyl, an ancient black castle. Of course, there are plenty of such views in Central Europe, but just this one—in the inexpressible and unique harmoniousness of its three principal parts, in its smile, in some mysterious innocence it had, my love! my obedient one!—was something so unique, and so familiar, and so long-promised, and it so *understood* the beholder that Vasili Ivanovich even pressed his hand to his heart, as if to see whether his heart was there in order to give it away.

At some distance, Schramm, poking into the air with the leader's alpenstock, was calling the attention of the excursionists to something or other; they had settled themselves around on the grass in poses seen in amateur snapshots, while the leader sat on a stump, his behind to the lake, and was having a snack. Quietly, concealing himself in his own shadow, Vasili Ivanovich followed the shore, and came to a kind of inn. A dog still quite young greeted him; it crept on its belly, its jaws laughing, its tail fervently beating the ground. Vasili Ivanovich accompanied the dog into the house, a piebald two-storied dwelling with a winking window beneath a convex tiled eyelid; and he found the owner, a tall old man vaguely resembling a Russian war veteran, who spoke German so poorly and with such a soft drawl that Vasili Ivanovich changed to his own tongue, but the man understood as in a dream and continued in the language of his environment, his family.

Upstairs was a room for travelers. "You know, I shall take it for the rest of my life," Vasili Ivanovich is reported to have said as soon as he had entered it. The room itself had nothing remarkable about it. On the contrary, it was a most ordinary room, with a red floor, daisies daubed on the white walls, and a small mirror half filled with the yellow infusion of the reflected flowers—but from the window one could clearly see the lake with its cloud and its castle, in a motionless and perfect correlation of happiness. Without reasoning, without considering, only entirely surrendering to an attraction the truth of which consisted in its own strength, a strength which he had never experienced before, Vasili Ivanovich in one radiant second realized that here in this little room with that view, beautiful to the verge of tears, life would at last be what he had always wished it to be. What exactly it would be like, what would take place here, that of course he did not know, but all around him were help, promise, and consolation—so that there could not be any doubt that he must live here. In a moment he figured out how he would manage it so as not to have to return to Berlin again, how to get the few possessions that he had—books, the blue suit, her photograph. How simple it was turning out! As my representative, he was earning enough for the modest life of a refugee Russian.

"My friends," he cried, having run down again to the meadow by the shore, "my friends, good-by. I shall remain for good in that house over there. We can't travel together any longer. I shall go no farther. I am not going anywhere. Good-by!"

"How is that?" said the leader in a queer voice, after a short pause, during which the smile on the lips of Vasili Ivanovich slowly faded, while the people who had been sitting on the grass half rose and stared at him with stony eyes.

"But why?" he faltered. "It is here that . . ."

"Silence!" the post-office clerk suddenly bellowed with extraordinary force. "Come to your senses, you drunken swine!"

"Wait a moment, gentlemen," said the leader, and, having passed his tongue over his lips, he turned to Vasili Ivanovich.

"You probably have been drinking," he said quietly. "Or have gone out of your mind. You are taking a pleasure trip with us. Tomorrow, according to the appointed itinerary—look at your ticket—we are all returning to Berlin. There can be no question of anyone—in this case you—refusing to continue this communal journey. We were singing today a certain song—try and remember what it said. That's enough now! Come, children, we are going on."

"There will be beer at Ewald," said Schramm in a caressing voice. "Five hours by train. Hikes. A hunting lodge. Coal mines. Lots of interesting things."

"I shall complain," wailed Vasili Ivanovich. "Give me back my bag. I have the right to remain where I want. Oh,

but this is nothing less than an invitation to a beheading"—
he told me he cried when they seized him by the arms.

"If necessary we shall carry you," said the leader grimly,
"but that is not likely to be pleasant. I am responsible for
each of you, and shall bring back each of you, alive or dead."

Swept along a forest road as in a hideous fairy tale,
squeezed, twisted, Vasili Ivanovich could not even turn
around, and only felt how the radiance behind his back
receded, fractured by trees, and then it was no longer there,
and all around the dark firs fretted but could not interfere.
As soon as everyone had got into the car and the train had
pulled off, they began to beat him—they beat him a long
time, and with a good deal of inventiveness. It occurred to
them, among other things, to use a corkscrew on his palms;
then on his feet. The post-office clerk, who had been to
Russia, fashioned a knout out of a stick and a belt, and
began to use it with devilish dexterity. Atta boy! The other
men relied more on their iron heels, whereas the women
were satisfied to pinch and slap. All had a wonderful time.

After returning to Berlin, he called on me, was much
changed, sat down quietly, putting his hands on his knees,
told his story; kept on repeating that he must resign his
position, begged me to let him go, insisted that he could
not continue, that he had not the strength to belong to man-
kind any longer. Of course, I let him go.

Marienbad, 1937.

Conversation Piece, 1945

I happen to have a disreputable namesake, complete from nickname to surname, a man whom I have never seen in the flesh but whose vulgar personality I have been able to deduce from his chance intrusions into the castle of my life. The tangle began in Prague, where I happened to be living in the middle twenties. A letter came to me there from a small library apparently attached to some sort of White Army organization which, like myself, had moved out of Russia. In exasperated tones, it demanded that I return at once a copy of the "Protocols of the Wise Men of Zion." This book, which in the old days had been wistfully appreciated by the Tsar, was a fake memorandum the secret police had paid a semiliterate crook to compile; its sole object was the promotion of pogroms. The librarian, who signed himself "Sinepuzov" (a surname, meaning "blue belly," which affects a Russian imagination in much the same way as Winterbottom does an English one), insisted that I had been keeping what he chose to call "this popular and valuable work" for more than a year. He referred to previous requests addressed to me in Belgrade, Berlin, and Brussels, through which towns my namesake apparently had been drifting.

I visualized the fellow as a young, very White émigré, of the automatically reactionary type, whose education had been interrupted by the revolution and who was successfully making up for lost time along traditional lines. He obviously was a great traveler; so was I—our only point in common. A Russian woman in Strasbourg asked me whether the man who had married her niece in Liège was my brother. One spring day, in Nice, a poker-faced girl with long earrings called at my hotel, asked to see me, took one look at me, apologized, and went away. In Paris, I received a telegram which jerkily ran, "NE VIENS PAS ALPHONSE DE RETOUR SOUPCONNE SOIS PRUDENT JE T'ADORE ANGOISSEE," and I admit deriving a certain grim satisfaction from the vision of my frivolous double inevitably bursting in, flowers in hand, upon Alphonse and his wife. A few years later, when I was lecturing in Zurich, I was suddenly arrested on a charge of smashing *three* mirrors in a restaurant—a kind of triptych featuring my namesake drunk (the first mirror), very drunk (the second), and roaring drunk (the third). Finally, in 1938, a French consul rudely refused to stamp my tattered sea-green Nansen passport because, he said, I had entered the country once before without a permit. In the fat dossier which was eventually produced, I caught a glimpse of my namesake's face. He had a clipped mustache and a crew haircut, the bastard.

When, soon after that, I came over to the United States

and settled down in Boston, I felt sure I had shaken off my absurd shadow. Then—last month, to be precise—there came a telephone call.

In a hard and glittering voice, a woman said she was Mrs. Sybil Hall, a close friend of Mrs. Sharp, who had written to her suggesting that she *contact* me. I did know a Mrs. Sharp and didn't stop to think that both my Mrs. Sharp and myself might not be the right ones. Golden-voiced Mrs. Hall said she was having a little meeting at her apartment Friday night and would I come, because she was sure from what she had heard about me that I would be very, very much interested in the discussion. Although meetings of any kind are loathsome to me, I was prompted to accept the invitation by the thought that if I did not I might·in some way disappoint Mrs. Sharp, a nice, maroon-trousered, short-haired old lady whom I had met on Cape Cod, where she shared a cottage with a younger woman; both ladies are mediocre Leftist artists of independent means, and completely amiable.

Owing to a misadventure, which had nothing to do with the subject of the present account, I arrived much later than I intended at Mrs. Hall's apartment house. An ancient elevator attendant, oddly resembling Richard Wagner, gloomily took me up, and Mrs. Hall's unsmiling maid, her long arms hanging down her sides, waited while I removed my overcoat and rubbers in the hall. Here the chief decorative note was a certain type of ornamental vase manufactured in China, and possibly of great antiquity—in this case a tall, sickly-colored brute of a thing—which always makes me abominably unhappy.

As I crossed a self-conscious, small room that fairly brimmed with symbols of what advertisement writers call "gracious living" and was being ushered—theoretically, for

the maid had dropped away—into a large, mellow, bourgeois salon, it gradually dawned upon me that this was
exactly the sort of place where one would expect to be
introduced to some old fool who had had caviar in the
Kremlin or to some wooden Soviet Russian, and that my
acquaintance Mrs. Sharp, who had for some reason always
resented my contempt for the Party line and for the Com-
munist and his Master's Voice, had decided, poor soul, that
such an experience might have a beneficial influence upon
my sacrilegious mind.

From a group of a dozen people, my hostess emerged in
the form of a long-limbed, flat-chested woman with lipstick on her prominent front teeth. She introduced me
rapidly to the guest of honor and her other guests, and the
discussion, which had been interrupted by my entrance,
was at once resumed. The guest of honor was answering
questions. He was a fragile-looking man with sleek, dark
hair and a glistening brow, and he was so brightly illu-
mined by the long-stalked lamp at his shoulder that one
could distinguish the specks of dandruff on the collar of
his dinner jacket and admire the whiteness of his clasped
hands, one of which I had found to be incredibly limp and
moist. He was the type of fellow whose weak chin, hollow
cheeks, and unhappy Adam's apple reveal, a couple of
hours after shaving, when the humble talcum powder has
worn off, a complex system of pink blotches overlaid with a
stipple of bluish gray. He wore a crested ring, and for some
odd reason I recalled a swarthy Russian girl in New York
who was so troubled by the possibility of being mistaken
for her notion of a Jewess that she used to wear a cross upon
her throat, although she had as little religion as brains.
The speaker's English was admirably fluent, but the hard
"djair" in his pronunciation of "Germany" and the persist-

ently recurring epithet "wonderful," the first syllable of which sounded like "wan," proclaimed his Teutonic origin. He was, or had been, or was to become, a professor of German, or music, or both, somewhere in the Middle West, but I did not catch his name and so shall call him Dr. Shoe.

"*Naturally* he was mad!" exclaimed Dr. Shoe in answer to something one of the ladies had asked. "Look, only a madman could have messed up the war the way he did. And I certainly hope, as you do, that before long, if he should turn out to be alive, he will be safely interned in a sanatorium somewhere in a neutral country. He has earned it. It was madness to attack Russia instead of invading England. It was madness to think that the war with Japan would prevent Roosevelt from participating energetically in European affairs. The worst madman is the one who fails to consider the possibility of somebody else's being mad, too."

"One cannot help feeling," said a fat little lady called, I think, Mrs. Mulberry, "that thousands of our boys who have been killed in the Pacific would still be alive if all those planes and tanks we gave England and Russia had been used to destroy Japan."

"Exactly," said Dr. Shoe. "And that was Adolf Hitler's mistake. Being mad, he failed to take into account the scheming of irresponsible politicians. Being mad, he believed that other governments would act in accordance with the principles of mercy and common sense."

"I always think of Prometheus," said Mrs. Hall, "Prometheus, who stole fire and was blinded by the angry gods."

An old lady in a bright-blue dress, who sat knitting in a corner, asked Dr. Shoe to explain why the Germans had not risen against Hitler.

Dr. Shoe lowered his eyelids for a moment. "The answer is a terrible one," he said with an effort. "As you know, I am German myself, of pure Bavarian stock, though a loyal citizen of this country. And nevertheless, I am going to say something very terrible about my former countrymen. Germans"—the soft-lashed eyes were half closed again—"Germans are dreamers."

By this time, of course, I had fully realized that Mrs. Hall's Mrs. Sharp was as totally distinct from my Mrs. Sharp as I was from my namesake. The nightmare into which I had been propelled would probably have struck him as a cozy evening with kindred souls, and Dr. Shoe might have seemed to him a most intelligent and brilliant *causeur*. Timidity, and perhaps morbid curiosity, kept me from leaving the room. Moreover, when I get excited, I stammer so badly that any attempt on my part to tell Dr. Shoe what I thought of him would have sounded like the explosions of a motorcycle which refuses to start on a frosty night in an intolerant suburban lane. I looked around, trying to convince myself that these were real people and not a Punch-and-Judy show.

None of the women were pretty; all had reached or over-reached forty-five. All, one could be certain, belonged to book clubs, bridge clubs, babble clubs, and to the great, cold sorority of inevitable death. All looked cheerfully sterile. Possibly some of them had had children, but how they had produced them was now a forgotten mystery; many had found substitutes for creative power in various aesthetic pursuits, such as, for instance, the beautifying of committee rooms. As I glanced at the one sitting next to me, an intense-looking lady with a freckled neck, I knew that, while patchily listening to Dr. Shoe, she was, in all probability, worrying about a bit of decoration having to do with some social event or wartime entertainment the exact nature of which I could not determine. But I did know how badly she needed that additional touch. "Something in the middle of the table," she was thinking. "I need something that would make people gasp—perhaps a great big huge bowl of artificial fruit. Not the wax kind, of course. Something nicely marbleized."

It is most regrettable that I did not fix the ladies' names in my mind when I was introduced to them. Two willowy, interchangeable maiden ladies on hard chairs had names beginning with "W," and, of the others, one was certainly called Miss Bissing. This I had heard distinctly, but could not later connect with any particular face or facelike object. There was only one other man besides Dr. Shoe and myself. He turned out to be a compatriot of mine, a Colonel Malikov or Melnikov; in Mrs. Hall's rendering it had sounded more like Milwaukee. While some soft, pale drinks were being passed around, he leaned toward me with a leathery, creaking sound, as if he wore a harness under his shabby blue suit, and informed me in a hoarse Russian whisper that he had had the honor of knowing my esteemed uncle, whom I at once visualized as a ruddy but unpalatable apple on my namesake's family tree. Dr. Shoe, however, was becoming eloquent again, and the Colonel straightened up, revealing a broken yellow tusk in his retreating smile and promising me by means of discreet gestures that we would have a good talk later on.

"The tragedy of Germany," said Dr. Shoe as he carefully folded the paper napkin with which he had wiped his thin lips, "is also the tragedy of cultured America. I have spoken at numerous women's clubs and other educational centers, and everywhere I have noted how deeply this European war, now mercifully ended, was loathed by refined, sensitive souls. I have also noted how eagerly cultured Americans revert in memory to happier days, to their traveling experiences abroad, to some unforgettable month or still more unforgettable year they once spent in the country of art, music, philosophy, and good humor. They remember the dear friends they had there, and their season of education and well-being in the bosom of a German nobleman's family, the exquisite cleanness of everything, the songs at the close of a perfect day, the wonderful little towns, and all that world of kindliness and romance they found in Munich or Dresden."

"*My* Dresden is no more," said Mrs. Mulberry. "Our bombs have destroyed it and everything it stands for."

"British ones, in this particular case," said Dr. Shoe gently. "But, of course, war is war, although I admit one finds it difficult to imagine German bombers deliberately selecting for their target some sacred historical spot in Pennsylvania or Virginia. Yes, war is terrible. In fact, it becomes almost intolerably so when it is forced upon two nations that have so many things in common. It may strike you as a paradox, but really, when one thinks of the soldiers slaughtered in Europe, one says to oneself that they are at least spared the terrible misgivings which we civilians must suffer in silence."

"I think th.. is very true," remarked Mrs. Hall, slowly nodding her head.

"What about those stories?" asked an old lady who was knitting. "Those stories the papers keep printing about the German atrocities. I suppose all that is mostly propaganda?"

Dr. Shoe smiled a tired smile. "I was expecting that question," he said with a touch of sadness in his voice. "Unfortunately, propaganda, exaggeration, faked photographs, and so on are the tools of modern war. I should not be surprised if the Germans themselves had made up stories about the cruelty of the American troops to innocent civilians. Just think of all the nonsense which was invented about the so-called German atrocities in the first World War—those horrible legends about Belgian women being seduced, and so on. Well, immediately after the war, in the summer of 1920, if I am not mistaken, a special committee of German democrats thoroughly investigated the whole matter, and we all know how pedantically thorough and precise German experts can be. Well, they did not find one scintilla of evidence to prove that Germans had not acted like soldiers and gentlemen."

One of the Misses W. ironically remarked that foreign correspondents must make a living. Her remark was witty. Everybody appreciated her ironical and witty remark.

"On the other hand," continued Dr. Shoe when the ripples had subsided, "let us forget propaganda for a moment and turn to dull facts. Allow me to draw you a little picture from the past, a rather sad little picture, but perhaps a necessary one. I will ask you to imagine German boys proudly entering some Polish or Russian town they had conquered. They sang as they marched. They did not know that their Fuhrer was mad; they innocently believed that they were bringing hope and happiness and wonderful order to the fallen town. They could not know that owing to subsequent mistakes and delusions on the part of Adolf Hitler, their conquest would eventually lead to the enemy's making a flaming battlefield of the very cities to which they, those German boys, thought they were bringing everlasting peace. As they bravely marched through the streets in all their finery, with their wonderful war machines and their banners, they smiled at everybody and everything because they were pathetically good-natured and well-meaning. They innocently expected the same friendly attitude on the part of the population Then, gradually, they realized that the streets through which they so boyishly, so confidently, marched were lined with silent and motionless crowds of Jews, who glared at them with hatred and who insulted each passing soldier, not by words—they were too clever for that—but by black looks and ill-concealed sneers."

"I know that kind of look," said Mrs. Hall grimly.

"But *they* did not," said Dr. Shoe in plaintive tones. "That is the point. They were puzzled. They did not understand, and they were hurt. So what did they do? At first they tried to fight that hatred with patient explanations and little tokens of kindness. But the wall of hatred surrounding them only got thicker. Finally they were forced to imprison the leaders of the vicious and arrogant coalition. What else could they do?"

"I happen to know an old Russian Jew," said Mrs. Mulberry. "Oh, just a business acquaintance of Mr. Mulberry's. Well, he confessed to me once that he would gladly strangle with his own hands the very first German soldier he met. I was so shocked that I just stood there and did not know what to answer."

"I would have," said a stout woman who sat with her knees wide apart. "As a matter of fact, one hears much too much about punishing the Germans. They, too, are human beings. And any sensitive person will agree with what you say about their not being responsible for those so-called atrocities, most of which have probably been invented by the Jews. I get mad when I hear people still jabbering about furnaces and torture houses which, if they existed at all, were operated by only a few men as insane as Hitler."

"Well, I am afraid one must be understanding," said Dr. Shoe, with his impossible smile, "and take into account the workings of the vivid Semitic imagination which controls the American press. And one must remember, too, that there were many purely sanitary measures which the orderly German troops had to adopt in dealing with the corpses of the elderly who had died in camp, and, in some cases, in disposing of the victims of typhus epidemics. I am quite free from any racial prejudices myself, and I can't see how these age-old racial problems have anything to do with the attitude to be adopted toward Germany now that she has surrendered. Especially when I remember the way the British treat natives in their colonies."

"Or how the Jewish Bolsheviks used to treat the Russian people—*ai-ai-ai!*" remarked Colonel Melnikov.

"Which is no more the case, is it?" asked Mrs. Hall.

"No, no," said the Colonel. "The great Russian people has waked up and my country is again a great country. We had three great leaders. We had Ivan, whom his enemies called Terrible, then we had Peter the Great, and now we have Joseph Stalin. I am a White Russian and have served in the Imperial Guards, but also I am a Russian patriot and a Russian Christian. Today, in every word that comes out of Russia, I feel the power, I feel the splendor of old Mother Russia. She is again a country of soldiers, religion, and true Slavs. Also, I know that when the Red Army entered German towns, not a single hair fell from German shoulders."

"Head," said Mrs. Hall.

"Yes," said the Colonel. "Not a single head from their shoulders."

"We all admire your countrymen," said Mrs. Mulberry. "But what about Communism spreading to Germany?"

"If I may be permitted to offer a suggestion," said Dr. Shoe, "I would like to point out that if we are not careful, there will be no Germany. The main problem which this country will have to face is to prevent the victors from enslaving the German nation and sending the young and hale and the lame and old—intellectuals and civilians—to work like convicts in the vast area of the East. This is against all the principles of democracy and war. If you tell me that the Germans did the same thing to the nations they conquered, I will remind you of three things: first, that the German State was not a democracy and couldn't be expected to act like one; secondly, that most, if not all, of the so-called 'slaves' came of their own free will; and in the third place—and this is the most important point—that they were well fed, well clothed, and lived in civilized surroundings which, in spite of all our natural enthusiasm for the immense population and geography of Russia, Germans are not likely to find in the country of the Soviets.

"Neither must we forget," continued Dr. Shoe, with a dramatic rise in his voice, "that Nazism was really not a German but an alien organization oppressing the German people. Adolf Hitler was an Austrian, Ley a Jew, Rosenberg half-French, half-Tartar. The German nation has suffered under this non-German yoke just as much as other European countries have suffered from the effects of the war waged on their soil. To civilians, who not only have been crippled and killed but whose treasured possessions and wonderful homes have been annihilated by bombs, it matters little whether those bombs were dropped by a German or an Allied plane. Germans, Austrians, Italians, Rumanians, Greeks, and all the other peoples of Europe are now members of one tragic brotherhood, all are equal in misery and hope, all should be treated alike, and let us leave the task of finding and judging the guilty to future historians, to unbiased old scholars in the immortal centers of European culture, in the serene universities of Heidelberg, Bonn, Jena, Leipzig, Munchen. Let the phoenix of Europe spread its eagle wings again, and God bless America."

There was a reverent pause while Dr. Shoe tremulously lighted a cigarette, and then Mrs. Hall, pressing the palms of her hands together in a charming, girlish gesture, begged him to round out the meeting with some lovely music. He sighed, got up, trod upon my foot in passing, apologetically touched my knee with the tips of his fingers, and, having sat down before the piano, bowed his head and remained motionless for several audibly silent seconds. Then, slowly and very gently, he laid his cigarette on an ash tray, removed the ash tray from the piano into Mrs. Hall's helpful hands, and bent his head again. At last he said, with a little catch in his voice, "First of all, I will play 'The Star-Spangled Banner.'"

Feeling that this was more than I could stand—in fact, having reached a point where I was beginning to feel physically sick—I got up and hurriedly left the room. As I was approaching the closet where I had seen the maid store my things, Mrs. Hall overtook me, together with a billow of distant music.

"Must you leave?" she said. "Must you really leave?"

I found my overcoat, dropped the hanger, and stamped into my rubbers.

"You are either murderers or fools," I said, "or both, and that man is a filthy German agent."

As I have already mentioned, I am afflicted with a bad stammer at crucial moments and therefore the sentence did not come out as smooth as it is on paper. But it worked. Before she could gather herself to answer, I had slammed the door behind me and was carrying my overcoat downstairs as one carries a child out of a house on fire. I was in the street when I noticed that the hat I was about to put on did not belong to me.

It was a well-worn fedora, of a deeper shade of gray than my own and with a narrower brim. The head it was meant for was smaller than mine. The inside of the hat carried the label "Werner Bros. Chicago" and smelled of another man's hairbrush and hair lotion. It could not belong to Colonel Melnikov, who was as bald as a bowling ball, and I assumed that Mrs. Hall's husband was either dead or kept his hats in another place. It was a disgusting object to carry about, but the night was rainy and cold, and I used the thing as a kind of rudimentary umbrella. As soon as I got home, I started writing a letter to the Federal Bureau of Investigation, but did not get very far. My inability to catch and retain names seriously impaired the quality of the information I was trying to impart, and since I had to explain my presence at the meeting, a lot of diffuse and vaguely suspicious matter concerning my own namesake had to be dragged in. Worst of all, the whole affair assumed a dreamlike, grotesque aspect when related in detail, whereas all I really had to say was that a person from some unknown address in the Middle West, a person whose name I did not even know, had been talking sympathetically about the German people to a group of silly old women in a private house. Indeed, judging by the expression of that same sympathy continuously cropping up in the writings of certain well-known columnists, the whole thing might be perfectly legal, for all I knew.

Early the next morning I opened the door in answer to a ring, and there was Dr. Shoe, bareheaded, raincoated, silently offering me my hat, with a cautious half-smile on his blue-and-pink face. I took the hat and mumbled some thanks. This he mistook for an invitation to come in. I could not remember where I had put his fedora, and the feverish search I had to conduct, more or less in his presence, soon became ludicrous.

"Look here," I said. "I shall mail, I shall send, I shall forward you that hat when I find it, or a check, if I don't."

"But I'm leaving this afternoon," he said gently, "and moreover, I would like to have a little explanation of the strange remark you addressed to my very dear friend Mrs. Hall."

He waited patiently while I tried to tell him as neatly as I could that the police, the authorities, would explain that to her.

"You do not understand," he said at length. "Mrs. Hall is a very well-known society lady and has numerous connections in official circles. Thank God we live in a great country, where everybody can speak his mind without being insulted for expressing a private opinion."

I told him to go away.

When my final splutter had petered out, he said, "I go away, but please remember, in this country—" and he shook his bent finger at me sidewise, German fashion, in facetious reproof.

Before I could decide where to hit him, he had glided out. I was trembling all over. My inefficiency, which at times has amused me and even pleased me in a subtle way, now appeared atrocious and base. All of a sudden I caught sight of Dr. Shoe's hat on a heap of old magazines under the little telephone table in my hall. I hurried to a front window, opened it, and, as Dr. Shoe emerged four stories below, tossed the hat in his direction. It described a parabola and made a pancake landing in the middle of the street. There it turned a somersault, missed a puddle by a matter of inches, and lay gaping, wrong side up. Dr. Shoe, without looking up, waved his hand in acknowledgment, retrieved the hat, satisfied himself that it was not too muddy, put it on, and walked away, jauntily wiggling his hips. I have often wondered why is it that a thin German always manages to look so plump behind when wearing a raincoat.

All that remains to be told is that a week later I received a letter the peculiar Russian of which can hardly be appreciated in translation.

"Esteemed Sir," it read. "You have been pursuing me all my life. Good friends of mine, after reading your books, have turned away from me thinking that I was the author of those depraved, decadent writings. In 1941, and again in 1943, I was arrested in France by the Germans for things I never had said or thought. Now in America, not content with having caused me all sorts of troubles in other countries, you have the arrogance to impersonate me and to appear in a drunken condition at the house of a highly respected person. This I will not tolerate. I could have you jailed and branded as an impostor, but I suppose you would not like that, and so I suggest that by way of indemnity . . ."

The sum he demanded was really a most modest one.

Boston, 1945.

"That in Aleppo Once..."

Dear V.—Among other things, this is to tell you that at last I am here, in the country whither so many sunsets have led. One of the first persons I saw was our good old Gleb Alexandrovich Gekko gloomily crossing Columbus Avenue in quest of the *petit café du coin* which none of us three will ever visit again. He seemed to think that somehow or other you were betraying our national literature, and he gave me your address with a deprecatory shake of his gray head, as if you did not deserve the treat of hearing from me.

I have a story for you. Which reminds me—I mean putting it like this reminds me—of the days when we wrote our first udder-warm bubbling verse, and all things, a rose, a puddle, a lighted window, cried out to us: "I'm a rhyme!" Yes, this is a most useful universe. We play, we die: *ig-rhyme, umi-rhyme*. And the sonorous souls of Russian verbs lend a meaning to the wild gesticulation of trees or to some discarded newspaper sliding and pausing, and shuffling again, with abortive flaps and apterous jerks along an endless wind-swept embankment. But just now I am not a poet. I come to you like that gushing lady in Chekhov who was dying to be described.

I married, let me see, about a month after you left France and a few weeks before the gentle Germans roared into Paris. Although I can produce documentary proofs of matrimony, I am positive now that my wife never existed. You may know her name from some other source, but that does not matter: it is the name of an illusion. Therefore, I am able to speak of her with as much detachment as I would of a character in a story (one of your stories, to be precise).

It was love at first touch rather than at first sight, for I had met her several times before without experiencing any special emotions; but one night, as I was seeing her home, something quaint she had said made me stoop with a laugh and lightly kiss her on the hair—and of course we all know of that blinding blast which is caused by merely picking up a small doll from the floor of a carefully abandoned house: the soldier involved hears nothing; for him it is but an ecstatic soundless and boundless expansion of what had been during his life a pin point of light in the dark center of his being. And really, the reason we think of death in celestial terms is that the visible firmament, especially at night (above our blacked-out Paris with the gaunt arches of its Boulevard Exelmans and the ceaseless Alpine gurgle of desolate latrines), is the most adequate and ever-present symbol of that vast silent explosion.

But I cannot discern her. She remains as nebulous as my best poem—the one you made such gruesome fun of in the *Literaturnïe Zapiski*. When I want to imagine her, I have to cling mentally to a tiny brown birthmark on her downy forearm, as one concentrates upon a punctuation mark in an illegible sentence. Perhaps, had she used a greater amount of make-up or used it more constantly, I might have visualized her face today, or at least the delicate transverse furrows of dry, hot rouged lips; but I fail, I fail—although I still feel their elusive touch now and then in the blindman's buff of my senses, in that sobbing sort of dream when she and I clumsily clutch at each other through a heartbreaking mist and I cannot see the color of her eyes for the blank luster of brimming tears drowning their irises.

She was much younger than I—not as much younger as was Nathalie of the lovely bare shoulders and long earrings in relation to swarthy Pushkin; but still there was a sufficient margin for that kind of retrospective romanticism which finds pleasure in imitating the destiny of a unique genius (down to the jealousy, down to the filth, down to the stab of seeing her almond-shaped eyes turn to her blond Cassio behind her peacock-feathered fan) even if one cannot imitate his verse. She liked mine though, and would scarcely have yawned as the other was wont to do every time her husband's poem happened to exceed the length of a sonnet. If she has remained a phantom to me, I may have been one to her: I suppose she had been solely attracted by the obscurity of my poetry; then tore a hole through its veil and saw a stranger's unlovable face.

As you know, I had been for some time planning to follow the example of your fortunate flight. She described to me an uncle of hers who lived, she said, in New York: he had taught riding at a Southern college and had wound up by marrying a wealthy American woman; they had a little daughter born deaf. She said she had lost their address long ago, but a few days later it miraculously turned up, and we wrote a dramatic letter to which we never received any reply. This did not much matter, as I had already obtained a sound affidavit from Professor Lomchenko of Chicago; but little else had been done in the way of getting the necessary papers, when the invasion began, whereas I foresaw that if we stayed on in Paris some helpful compatriot of mine would sooner or later point out to the interested party sundry passages in one of my books where I argued that, with all her many black sins, Germany was still bound to remain forever and ever the laughing stock of the world.

So we started upon our disastrous honeymoon. Crushed and jolted amid the apocalyptic exodus, waiting for unscheduled trains that were bound for unknown destinations, walking through the stale stage setting of abstract towns, living in a permanent twilight of physical exhaustion, we fled; and the farther we fled, the clearer it became that what was driving us on was something more than a booted and buckled fool with his assortment of variously propelled junk—something of which he was a mere symbol, something monstrous and impalpable, a timeless and faceless mass of immemorial horror that still keeps coming at me from behind even here, in the green vacuum of Central Park.

Oh, she bore it gamely enough—with a kind of dazed cheerfulness. Once, however, quite suddenly she started to sob in a sympathetic railway carriage. "The dog," she said, "the dog we left. I cannot forget the poor dog." The honesty of her grief shocked me, as we had never had any dog. "I know," she said, "but I tried to imagine we had actually bought that setter. And just think, he would be now whining behind a locked door." There had never been any talk of buying a setter.

I should also not like to forget a certain stretch of highroad and the sight of a family of refugees (two women, a child) whose old father, or grandfather, had died on the way. The sky was a chaos of black and flesh-colored clouds with an ugly sunburst beyond a hooded hill, and the dead man was lying on his back under a dusty plane tree. With a stick and their hands the women had tried to dig a road-side grave, but the soil was too hard; they had given it up and were sitting side by side, among the anemic poppies, a little apart from the corpse and its upturned beard. But the little boy was still scratching and scraping and tugging until he tumbled a flat stone and forgot the object of his solemn exertions as he crouched on his haunches, his thin, eloquent neck showing all its vertebrae to the headsman, and watched with surprise and delight thousands of minute brown ants seething, zigzagging, dispersing, heading for places of safety in the Gard, and the Aude, and the Drome, and the Var, and the Basses-Pyrénées—we two paused only in Pau.

Spain proved too difficult and we decided to move on to Nice. At a place called Faugères (a ten-minute stop) I squeezed out of the train to buy some food. When a couple of minutes later I came back, the train was gone, and the muddled old man responsible for the atrocious void that faced me (coal dust glittering in the heat between naked indifferent rails, and a lone piece of orange peel) brutally told me that, anyway, I had had no right to get out.

In a better world I could have had my wife located and told what to do (I had both tickets and most of the money); as it was, my nightmare struggle with the telephone proved futile, so I dismissed the whole series of diminutive voices barking at me from afar, sent two or three telegrams which are probably on their way only now, and late in the evening took the next local to Montpellier, farther than which her train would not stumble. Not finding her there, I had to choose between two alternatives: going on because she might have boarded the Marseilles train which I had just missed, or going back because she might have returned to Faugères. I forgot now what tangle of reasoning led me to Marseilles and Nice.

Beyond such routine action as forwarding false data to a few unlikely places, the police did nothing to help: one man bellowed at me for being a nuisance; another sidetracked the question by doubting the authenticity of my marriage certificate because it was stamped on what he contended to be the wrong side; a third, a fat *commissaire* with liquid brown eyes confessed that he wrote poetry in his spare time. I looked up various acquaintances among the numerous Russians domiciled or stranded in Nice. I heard those among them who chanced to have Jewish blood talk of their doomed kinsmen crammed into hell-bound trains; and my own plight, by contrast, acquired a commonplace air of irreality while I sat in some crowded café with the milky blue sea in front of me and a shell-hollow murmur behind telling and retelling the tale of massacre and misery, and the gray paradise beyond the ocean, and the ways and whims of harsh consuls.

A week after my arrival an indolent plain-clothes man called upon me and took me down a crooked and smelly street to a black-stained house with the word "hotel" almost erased by dirt and time; there, he said, my wife had been found. The girl he produced was an absolute stranger, of course; but my friend Holmes kept on trying for some time to make her and me confess we were married, while her taciturn and muscular bedfellow stood by and listened, his bare arms crossed on his striped chest.

When at length I got rid of those people and had wandered back to my neighborhood, I happened to pass by a compact queue waiting at the entrance of a food store; and there, at the very end, was my wife, straining on tiptoe to catch a glimpse of what exactly was being sold. I think the first thing she said to me was that she hoped it was oranges.

Her tale seemed a trifle hazy, but perfectly banal. She had returned to Faugères and gone straight to the Commissariat instead of making inquiries at the station, where I had left a message for her. A party of refugees suggested that she join them; she spent the night in a bicycle shop with no bicycles, on the floor, together with three elderly women who lay, she said, like three logs in a row. Next day she realized that she had not enough money to reach Nice. Eventually she borrowed some from one of the log-women. She got into the wrong train, however, and traveled to a town the name of which she could not remember. She had arrived at Nice two days ago and had found some friends at the Russian church. They had told her I was somewhere around, looking for her, and would surely turn up soon.

Some time later, as I sat on the edge of the only chair in my garret and held her by her slender young hips (she was combing her soft hair and tossing her head back with every stroke), her dim smile changed all at once into an odd quiver and she placed one hand on my shoulder, staring down at me as if I were a reflection in a pool, which she had noticed for the first time.

"I've been lying to you, dear," she said. "*Ya lgunia*. I stayed for several nights in Montpellier with a brute of a man I met on the train. I did not want it at all. He sold hair lotions."

The time, the place, the torture. Her fan, her gloves, her mask. I spent that night and many others getting it out of her bit by bit, but not getting it all. I was under the strange

147

delusion that first I must find out every detail, reconstruct every minute, and only then decide whether I could bear it. But the limit of desired knowledge was unattainable, nor could I ever foretell the approximate point after which I might imagine myself satiated, because of course the denominator of every fraction of knowledge was potentially as infinite as the number of intervals between the fractions themselves.

Oh, the first time she had been too tired to mind, and the next had not minded because she was sure I had deserted her; and she apparently considered that such explanations ought to be a kind of consolation prize for me instead of the nonsense and agony they really were. It went on like that for eons, she breaking down every now and then, but soon rallying again, answering my unprintable questions in a breathless whisper or trying with a pitiful smile to wriggle into the semisecurity of irrelevant commentaries, and I crushing and crushing the mad molar till my jaw almost burst with pain, a flaming pain which seemed somehow preferable to the dull, humming ache of humble endurance.

And mark, in between the periods of this inquest, we were trying to get from reluctant authorities certain papers which in their turn would make it lawful to apply for a third kind which would serve as a steppingstone towards a permit enabling the holder to apply for yet other papers which might or might not give him the means of discovering how and why it had happened. For even if I could imagine the accursed recurrent scene, I failed to link up its sharp-angled grotesque shadows with the dim limbs of my wife as she shook and rattled and dissolved in my violent grasp.

So nothing remained but to torture each other, to wait for hours on end in the Prefecture, filling forms, conferring with friends who had already probed the innermost viscera of all visas, pleading with secretaries, and filling forms again, with the result that her lusty and versatile traveling salesman became blended in a ghastly mix-up with rat-whiskered snarling officials, rotting bundles of obsolete records, the reek of violet ink, bribes slipped under gangrenous blotting paper, fat flies tickling moist necks with their rapid cold padded feet, new-laid clumsy concave photographs of your six subhuman doubles, the tragic eyes and patient politeness of petitioners born in Slutzk, Starodub, or Bobruisk, the funnels and pulleys of the Holy Inquisition, the awful smile of the bald man with the glasses, who had been told that his passport could not be found.

I confess that one evening, after a particularly abominable day, I sank down on a stone bench weeping and cursing a mock world where millions of lives were being juggled by the clammy hands of consuls and *commissaires*. I noticed she was crying too, and then I told her that nothing would really have mattered the way it mattered now, had she not gone and done what she did.

"You will think me crazy," she said with a vehemence that, for a second, almost made a real person of her, "but I didn't—I swear that I didn't. Perhaps I live several lives at once. Perhaps I wanted to test you. Perhaps this bench is a dream and we are in Saratov or on some star."

It would be tedious to niggle the different stages through which I passed before accepting finally the first version of her delay. I did not talk to her and was a good deal alone. She would glimmer and fade, and reappear with some trifle she thought I would appreciate—a handful of cherries, three precious cigarettes or the like—treating me with the unruffled mute sweetness of a nurse that trips from and to a gruff convalescent. I ceased visiting most of our mutual friends because they had lost all interest in my passport affairs and seemed to have turned vaguely inimical. I composed several poems. I drank all the wine I could get. I clasped her one day to my groaning breast, and we went for a week to Caboule and lay on the round pink pebbles of the narrow beach. Strange to say, the happier our new relations seemed, the stronger I felt an undercurrent of poignant sadness, but I kept telling myself that this was an intrinsic feature of all true bliss.

In the meantime, something had shifted in the moving pattern of our fates and at last I emerged from a dark and hot office with a couple of plump *visas de sortie* cupped in my trembling hands. Into these the U.S.A. serum was duly injected, and I dashed to Marseilles and managed to get tickets for the very next boat. I returned and tramped up the stairs. I saw a rose in a glass on the table—the sugar pink of its obvious beauty, the parasitic air bubbles clinging to its stem. Her two spare dresses were gone, her comb was gone, her checkered coat was gone, and so was the mauve hairband with a mauve bow that had been her hat. There was no note pinned to the pillow, nothing at all in the room to enlighten me, for of course the rose was merely what French rhymsters call *une cheville*.

I went to the Veretennikovs, who could tell me nothing; to the Hellmans, who refused to say anything; and to the Elagins, who were not sure whether to tell me or not. Finally the old lady—and you know what Anna Vladimirovna is like at crucial moments—asked for her rubber-tipped cane, heavily but energetically dislodged her bulk from her favorite armchair, and took me into the garden. There she informed me that, being twice my age, she had the right to say I was a bully and a cad.

You must imagine the scene: the tiny graveled garden with its blue Arabian Nights jar and solitary cypress; the cracked terrace where the old lady's father had dozed with a rug on his knees when he retired from his Novgorod governorship to spend a few last evenings in Nice; the pale-green sky; a whiff of vanilla in the deepening dusk; the crickets emitting their metallic trill pitched at two octaves above middle C; and Anna Vladimirovna, the folds of her cheeks jerkily dangling as she flung at me a motherly but quite undeserved insult.

During several preceding weeks, my dear V., every time she had visited by herself the three or four families we both knew, my ghostly wife had filled the eager ears of all those kind people with an extraordinary story. To wit: that she had madly fallen in love with a young Frenchman who could give her a turreted home and a crested name; that she had implored me for a divorce and I had refused; that in fact I had said I would rather shoot her and myself than sail to New York alone; that she had said her father in a similar case had acted like a gentleman; that I had answered I did not give a hoot for her *cocu de père*.

There were loads of other preposterous details of the kind—but they all hung together in such a remarkable fashion that no wonder the old lady made me swear I would not seek to pursue the lovers with a cocked pistol. They had gone, she said, to a château in Lozère. I inquired whether she had ever set eyes upon the man. No, but she had been shown his picture. As I was about to leave, Anna Vladimirovna, who had slightly relaxed and had even given me her five fingers to kiss, suddenly flared up again, struck the gravel with her cane, and said in her deep strong voice: "But one thing I shall never forgive you—her dog, that poor beast which you hanged with your own hands before leaving Paris."

Whether the gentleman of leisure had changed into a

traveling salesman, or whether the metamorphosis had been reversed, or whether again he was neither the one nor the other, but the nondescript Russian who had courted her before our marriage—all this was absolutely inessential. She had gone. That was the end. I should have been a fool had I begun the nightmare business of searching and waiting for her all over again.

On the fourth morning of a long and dismal sea voyage, I met on the deck a solemn but pleasant old doctor with whom I had played chess in Paris. He asked me whether my wife was very much incommoded by the rough seas. I answered that I had sailed alone; whereupon he looked taken aback and then said he had seen her a couple of days before going on board, namely in Marseilles, walking, rather aimlessly he thought, along the embankment. She said that I would presently join her with bag and tickets.

This is, I gather, the point of the whole story—although if you write it, you had better not make him a doctor, as that kind of thing has been overdone. It was at that moment that I suddenly knew for certain that she had never existed at all. I shall tell you another thing. When I arrived I hastened to satisfy a certain morbid curiosity: I went to the address she had given me once; it proved to be an anonymous gap between two office buildings; I looked for her uncle's name in the directory; it was not there; I made some inquiries, and Gekko, who knows everything, informed me that the man and his horsey wife existed all right, but had moved to San Francisco after their deaf little girl had died.

Viewing the past graphically, I see our mangled romance engulfed in a deep valley of mist between the crags of two matter-of-fact mountains: life had been real before, life will be real from now on, I hope. Not tomorrow, though.

Perhaps after tomorrow. You, happy mortal, with your lovely family (how is Ines? how are the twins?) and your diversified work (how are the lichens?), can hardly be expected to puzzle out my misfortune in terms of human communion, but you may clarify things for me through the prism of your art.

Yet the pity of it. Curse your art, I am hideously unhappy. She keeps on walking to and fro where the brown nets are spread to dry on the hot stone slabs and the dappled light of the water plays on the side of a moored fishing boat. Somewhere, somehow, I have made some fatal mistake. There are tiny pale bits of broken fish scales glistening here and there in the brown meshes. It may all end in *Aleppo* if I am not careful. Spare me, V.: you would load your dice with an unbearable implication if you took that for a title.

Boston, 1943.

Time and Ebb

1

In the first floriferous days of convalescence after a severe illness, which nobody, least of all the patient himself, expected a ninety-year-old organism to survive, I was admonished by my dear friends Norman and Nura Stone to prolong the lull in my scientific studies and relax in the midst of some innocent occupation such as brazzle or solitaire.

The first is out of the question, since tracking the name of an Asiatic town or the title of a Spanish novel through a maze of jumbled syllables on the last page of the evening newsbook (a feat which my youngest great-granddaughter performs with the utmost zest) strikes me as far more strenuous than toying with animal tissues. Solitaire, on the other hand, is worthy of consideration, especially if one is sensitive to its mental counterpart; for is not the setting down of one's reminiscences a game of the same order, wherein events and emotions are dealt to oneself in leisurely retrospection?

Arthur Freeman is reported to have said of memoirists that they are men who have too little imagination to write fiction and too bad a memory to write the truth. In this twilight of self-expression I too must float. Like other old men before me, I have discovered that the near in time is annoyingly confused, whereas at the end of the tunnel there are color and light. I can discern the features of every month in 1944 or 1945, but seasons are utterly blurred when I pick out 1997 or 2012. I cannot remember the name of the eminent scientist who attacked my latest paper, as I have also forgotten those other names which my equally eminent defenders called him. I am unable to tell offhand what year the Embryological Section of the Association of Nature Lovers of Reykjavik elected me a corresponding member, or when, exactly, the American Academy of Science awarded me its choicest prize. (I remember, though, the keen pleasure which both these honors gave me.) Thus a man looking through a tremendous telescope does not see the cirri of an Indian summer above his charmed orchard, but does see, as my regretted colleague, the late Professor Alexander Ivanchenko, twice saw, the swarming of hesperozoa in a humid valley of the planet Venus.

No doubt the "numberless nebulous pictures" bequeathed us by the drab, flat, and strangely melancholic photography of the past century exaggerate the impression of unreality which that century makes upon those who do not remember it; but the fact remains that the beings that peopled the world in the days of my childhood seem to the present generation more remote than the nineteenth century seemed to them. They were still up to their waists in its prudery and prejudice. They clung to tradition as a vine still clings to a dead tree. They had their meals at large tables around which they grouped themselves in a stiff sitting position on hard wooden chairs. Clothes consisted of a number of parts, each of which, moreover, contained the reduced and useless remnants of this or that older fashion (a townsman dressing of a morning had to squeeze something like thirty buttons into as many buttonholes besides tying three knots and checking the contents of fifteen pockets).

In their letters they addressed perfect strangers by what was—insofar as words have sense—the equivalent of "beloved master" and prefaced a theoretically immortal signature with a mumble expressing idiotic devotion to a person whose very existence was to the writer a matter of complete unconcern. They were atavistically prone to endow the community with qualities and rights which they refused to the individual. Economics obsessed them almost as much as theologies had obsessed their ancestors. They were superficial, careless, and shortsighted. More than other generations, they tended to overlook outstanding men, leaving to us the honor of discovering their classics (thus Richard Sinatra remained, while he lived, an anonymous "ranger" dreaming under a Telluride pine or reading his prodigious verse to the squirrels of San Isabel Forest, whereas everybody knew another Sinatra, a minor writer, also of Oriental descent).

Elementary allobiotic phenomena led their so-called spiritualists to the silliest forms of transcendental surmise and made so-called common sense shrug its broad shoulders in equally silly ignorance. Our denominations of time would have seemed to them "telephone" numbers. They played with electricity in various ways without having the slightest notion of what it really was—and no wonder the chance revelation of its true nature came as a most hideous surprise (I was a man by that time and can well remember old Professor Andrews sobbing his heart out on the campus in the midst of a dumbfounded crowd).

But in spite of all the ridiculous customs and complications in which it was entangled, the world of my young days was a gallant and tough little world that countered adversity with a bit of dry humor and would calmly set out for remote battlefields in order to suppress the savage vulgarity of Hitler or Alamillo. And if I let myself go, many would be the bright, and kind, and dreamy, and lovely things which impassioned memory would find in the past—and then woe to the present age, for there is no knowing what a still vigorous old man might do to it if he tucked up his sleeves. But enough of this. History is not my field, so perhaps I had better turn to the personal lest I be told, as Mr. Saskatchewanov is told by the most charming character in present-day fiction (corroborated by my great-granddaughter, who reads more than I do), that "ev'ry cricket ought keep to its picket"—and not intrude on the rightful domain of other "gads and summersmiths."

2

I was born in Paris. My mother died when I was still an infant, so that I can only recall her as a vague patch of delicious lachrymal warmth just beyond the limit of iconographic memory. My father taught music and was a composer himself (I still treasure an ancient program where his name stands next to that of a great Russian); he saw me through my college stage and died of an obscure blood disease at the time of the South American War.

I was in my seventh year when he and I, and the sweetest

grandmother a child has ever been blessed with, left Europe, where indescribable tortures were being inflicted by a degenerate nation upon the race to which I belong. A woman in Portugal gave me the hugest orange I had ever seen. From the stern of the liner two small cannon covered its portentously tortuous wake. A party of dolphins performed solemn somersaults. My grandmother read me a tale about a mermaid who had acquired a pair of feet. The inquisitive breeze would join in the reading and roughly finger the pages so as to discover what was going to happen next. That is about all I remember of the voyage.

Upon reaching New York, travelers in space used to be as much impressed as travelers in time would have been by the old-fashioned "skyscrapers"; this was a misnomer, since their association with the sky, especially at the ethereal close of a greenhouse day, far from suggesting any grating contact, was indescribably delicate and serene: to my childish eyes looking across the vast expanse of park land that used to grace the center of the city, they appeared remote and lilac-colored, and strangely aquatic, mingling as they did their first cautious lights with the colors of the sunset and revealing, with a kind of dreamy candor, the pulsating inside of their semitransparent structure.

Negro children sat quietly upon the artificial rocks. The trees had their Latin binomials displayed upon their trunks, just as the drivers of the squat, gaudy, scaraboid motorcabs (generically allied in my mind to certain equally gaudy automatic machines upon the musical constipation of which the insertion of a small coin used to act as a miraculous laxative) had their stale photographic pictures affixed to their backs; for we lived in the era of Identification and Tabulation; saw the personalities of men and things in terms of names and nicknames and did not believe in the existence of anything that was nameless.

In a recent and still popular play dealing with the quaint America of the Flying Forties, a good deal of glamour is infused into the part of the Soda Jerk, but the side whiskers and the starched shirt front are absurdly anachronistic, nor was there in my day such a continuous and violent revolving of tall mushroom seats as is indulged in by the performers. We imbibed our humble mixtures (through straws that were really much shorter than those employed on the stage) in an atmosphere of gloomy greed. I remember the shallow enchantment and the minor poetry of the proceedings: the copious froth engendered above the sunken lump of frozen synthetic cream, or the liquid brown mud of "fudge" sauce poured over its polar pate. Brass and glass surfaces, sterile reflections of electric lamps, the whirr and shimmer of a caged propeller, a Global War poster depicting Uncle Sam and his Rooseveltian tired blue eyes or else a dapper uniformed girl with a hypertrophied nether lip (that pout, that sullen kiss-trap, that transient fashion in feminine charm—1939–1950), and the unforgettable tonality of mixed traffic noises coming from the street—these patterns and melodic figures, for the conscious analysis of which time is alone responsible, somehow connected the "drugstore" with a world where men tormented metals and where metals hit back.

I attended a school in New York; then we moved to Boston; and then we moved again. We seem always to have been shifting quarters—and some homes were duller than others; but no matter how small the town, I was sure to find a place where bicycle tires were repaired, and a place where ice cream was sold, and a place where cinematographic pictures were shown.

Mountain gorges seemed to have been ransacked for echoes; these were subjected to a special treatment on a basis of honey and rubber until their condensed accents could be synchronized with the labial movements of serial photographs on a moon-white screen in a velvet-dark hall. With a blow of his fist a man sent a fellow creature crashing into a tower of crates. An incredibly smooth-skinned girl raised a linear eyebrow. A door slammed with the kind of ill-fitting thud that comes to us from the far bank of a river where woodsmen are at work.

3

I am also old enough to remember the coach trains: as a babe I worshiped them; as a boy I turned away to improved editions of speed. With their haggard windows and dim lights they still lumber sometimes through my dreams. Their hue might have passed for the ripeness of distance, for a blending succession of conquered miles, had it not surrendered its plum-bloom to the action of coal dust so as to match the walls of workshops and slums which preceded a city as inevitably as a rule of grammar and a blot precede the acquisition of conventional knowledge. Dwarf dunce caps were stored at one end of the car and could flabbily cup (with the transmission of a diaphanous chill to the fingers) the grottolike water of an obedient little fountain which reared its head at one's touch.

Old men resembling the hoary ferryman of still more ancient fairy tales chanted out their intermittent "next-ations" and checked the tickets of the travelers, among whom there were sure to be, if the journey was reasonably long, a great number of sprawling, dead-tired soldiers and one live, drunken soldier, tremendously peripatetic and with only his pallor to connect him with death. He always occurred singly but he was always there, a freak, a young creature of clay, in the midst of what some very modern history textbooks glibly call Hamilton's period—after the indifferent scholar who put that period into shape for the benefit of the brainless.

Somehow or other my brilliant but unpractical father never could adapt himself to academic conditions sufficiently to stay very long in this or that place. I can visualize all of them, but one college town remains especially vivid: there is no need to name it if I say that three lawns from us, in a leafy lane, stood the house which is now the Mecca of a nation. I remember the sun-splashed garden chairs under the apple tree, and a bright copper-colored setter, and a fat, freckled boy with a book in his lap, and a handy-looking apple that I picked up in the shadow of a hedge.

And I doubt whether the tourists who nowadays visit the birthplace of the greatest man of his time and peer at the period furniture self-consciously huddled beyond the plush ropes of enshrined immortality can feel anything of that proud contact with the past which I owe to a chance incident. For whatever happens, and no matter how many index cards librarians may fill with the titles of my published papers, I shall go down to posterity as the man who had once thrown an apple at Barrett.

To those who have been born since the staggering discoveries of the seventies, and who thus have seen nothing in the nature of flying things save perhaps a kite or a toy balloon (still permitted, I understand, in several states in spite of Dr. de Sutton's recent articles on the subject), it is not easy to imagine airplanes, particularly because old photographic pictures of those splendid machines in full flight lack the life which only art could have been capable of retaining—and oddly enough no great painter ever chose them as a special subject into which to inject his genius and thus preserve their image from deterioration.

I suppose I am old-fashioned in my attitude towards many aspects of life that happen to be outside my particular branch of science; and possibly the personality of the very old man I am may seem divided, like those little European towns one half of which is in France and the other in Russia. I know this and proceed warily. Far from me is the intention to promote any yearning and morbid regret in regard to flying machines, but at the same time I cannot suppress the romantic undertone which is inherent to the symphonic entirety of the past as I feel it.

In those distant days when no spot on earth was more than sixty hours' flying time from one's local airport, a boy would know planes from propeller spinner to rudder trim tab, and could distinguish the species not only by the shape of the wing tip or the jutting of a cockpit, but even by the pattern of exhaust flames in the darkness; thus vying in the recognition of characters with those mad nature-sleuths —the post-Linnean systematists. A sectional diagram of wing and fuselage construction would give him a stab of creative delight, and the models he wrought of balsa and pine and paper clips provided such increasing excitement during the making that, by comparison, their completion seemed almost insipid, as if the spirit of the thing had flown away at the moment its shape had become fixed.

Attainment and science, retainment and art—the two couples keep to themselves, but when they do meet, nothing else in the world matters. And so I shall tiptoe away, taking leave of my childhood at its most typical point, in its most plastic posture: arrested by a deep drone that vibrates and gathers in volume overhead, stock-still, oblivious of the meek bicycle it straddles, one foot on the pedal, the toe of the other touching the asphalted earth, eyes, chin, and ribs lifted to the naked sky where a war plane comes with unearthly speed which only the expanse of its medium renders unhurried as ventral view changes to rear view, and wings and hum dissolve in the distance. Admirable monsters, great flying machines, they have gone, they have vanished like that flock of swans which passed with a mighty swish of multitudinous wings one spring night above Knights Lake in Maine, from the unknown into the unknown: swans of a species never determined by science, never seen before, never seen since—and then nothing but a lone star remained in the sky, like an asterisk leading to an undiscoverable footnote.

Boston, 1945.

Scenes from the Life of a Double Monster

Some years ago Dr. Fricke asked Lloyd and me a question that I shall try to answer now. With a dreamy smile of scientific delectation he stroked the fleshy cartilaginous band uniting us—*omphalopagus diaphragmo-xiphodidymus*, as Pancoast has dubbed a similar case—and wondered if we could recall the very first time either of us, or both, realized the peculiarity of our condition and destiny. All Lloyd could remember was the way our Grandfather Ibrahim (or Ahim, or Ahem—irksome lumps of dead sounds to the ear of today!) would touch what the doctor was touching and call it a bridge of gold. I said nothing.

Our childhood was spent atop a fertile hill above the Black Sea on our grandfather's farm near Karaz. His youngest daughter, rose of the East, gray Ahem's pearl (if so, the old scoundrel might have taken better care of her) had been raped in a roadside orchard by our anonymous sire and had died soon after giving birth to us—of sheer horror and grief, I imagine. One set of rumors mentioned a Hungarian peddler; another favored a German collector of birds or some member of his expedition—his taxidermist, most likely. Dusky, heavily necklaced aunts, whose voluminous clothes smelled of rose oil and mutton, attended with ghoulish zest to the wants of our monstrous infancy.

Soon neighboring hamlets learned the astounding news and began delegating to our farm various inquisitive strangers. On feast days you could see them laboring up the slopes of our hill, like pilgrims in bright-colored pictures. There was a shepherd seven feet tall, and a small bald man with glasses, and soldiers, and the lengthening shadows of cypresses. Children came too, at all times, and were shooed away by our jealous nurses; but almost daily some black-eyed, cropped-haired youngster in dark-patched, faded-blue pants would manage to worm his way through the dogwood, the honeysuckle, the twisted Judas trees, into the cobbled court with its old rheumy fountain where little Lloyd and Floyd (we had other names then, full of corvine aspirates—but no matter) sat quietly munching dried apricots under a whitewashed wall. Then, suddenly, the aitch would see an eye, the Roman two a one, the scissors a knife.

There can be, of course, no comparison between this impact of knowledge, disturbing as it may have been, and the emotional shock my mother received (by the way, what clean bliss there is in this deliberate use of the possessive singular!). She must have been aware that she was being delivered of twins; but when she learned, as no doubt she did, that the twins were conjoined ones—what did she experience then? With the kind of unrestrained, ignorant, passionately communicative folks that surrounded us, the highly vocal household just beyond the limits of her tumbled bed must, surely, have told her at once that something had gone dreadfully wrong; and one can be certain that her sisters, in the frenzy of their fright and compassion, showed her the double baby. I am not saying that a mother cannot love such a double thing—and forget in this love the dark dews of its unhallowed origin; I only think that the mixture of revulsion, pity, and a mother's love was too much for her. Both components of the double series before her staring eyes were healthy, handsome little components, with a silky fair fuzz on their violet-pink skulls, and well-formed rubbery arms and legs that moved like the many limbs of some wonderful sea animal. Each was eminently normal, but together they formed a monster. Indeed, it is strange to think that the presence of a mere band of tissue, a flap of flesh not much longer than a lamb's liver, should be able to transform joy, pride, tenderness, adoration, gratitude to God into horror and despair.

In our own case, everything was far simpler. Adults were much too different from us in all respects to afford any analogy, but our first coeval visitor was to me a mild revelation. While Lloyd placidly contemplated the awe-struck child of seven or eight who was peering at us from under a humped and likewise peering fig tree, I remember appreciating in full the essential difference between the newcomer and me. He cast a short blue shadow on the ground, and so did I; but in addition to that sketchy, and flat, and unstable companion which he and I owed to the sun and which vanished in dull weather I possessed yet another shadow, a palpable reflection of my corporal self, that I always had by me, at my left side, whereas my visitor had somehow managed to lose his, or had unhooked it and left it at home. Linked Lloyd and Floyd were complete and normal; he was neither.

But perhaps, in order to elucidate these matters as thoroughly as they deserve, I should say something of still earlier recollections. Unless adult emotions stain past ones, I think I can vouch for the memory of a faint disgust. By virtue of our anterior duplexity, we lay originally front to front, joined at our common navel, and my face in those first years of our existence was constantly brushed by my twin's hard nose and wet lips. A tendency to throw our heads back and avert our faces as much as possible was a natural reaction to those bothersome contacts. The great flexibility of our band of union allowed us to assume reciprocally a more or less lateral position, and as we learned to walk we waddled about in this side-by-side attitude, which must have seemed more strained than it really was, making us look, I suppose, like a pair of drunken dwarfs supporting each other. For a long time we kept reverting in sleep to our fetal position; but whenever the discomfort it engendered woke us up, we would again jerk our faces away, in regardant revulsion, with a double wail.

I insist that at three or four our bodies obscurely disliked their clumsy conjunction, while our minds did not question its normalcy. Then, before we could have become mentally aware of its drawbacks, physical intuition discovered means of tempering them, and thereafter we hardly gave them a thought. All our movements became a judicious compromise between the common and the particular. The pattern of acts prompted by this or that mutual urge formed a kind of gray, evenly woven, generalized background against which the discrete impulse, his or mine, followed a brighter and sharper course; but (guided as it were by the warp of the background pattern) it never went athwart the common weave or the other twin's whim.

I am speaking at present solely of our childhood, when nature could not yet afford to have us undermine our hard-won vitality by any conflict between us. In later years I have had occasion to regret that we did not perish or had not been surgically separated, before we left that initial stage at which an ever-present rhythm, like some kind of remote tom-tom beating in the jungle of our nervous system, was alone responsible for the regulation of our movements. When, for example, one of us was about to stoop to possess himself of a pretty daisy and the other, at exactly the same moment, was on the point of stretching up to pluck a ripe fig, individual success depended upon whose movement happened to conform to the current ictus of our common and continuous rhythm, whereupon, with a very brief, chorealike shiver, the interrupted gesture of one twin would be swallowed and dissolved in the enriched ripple of the other's completed action. I say "enriched" because the ghost of the unpicked flower somehow seemed to be also there, pulsating between the fingers that closed upon the fruit.

There might be a period of weeks and even months when the guiding beat was much more often on Lloyd's side than on mine, and then a period might follow when I would be on top of the wave; but I cannot recall any time in our childhood when frustration or success in these matters provoked in either of us resentment or pride.

Somewhere within me, however, there must have been some sensitive cell wondering at the curious fact of a force that would suddenly sweep me away from the object of a casual desire and drag me to other, uncoveted things that were thrust into the sphere of my will instead of being consciously reached for and enveloped by its tentacles. So, as I watched this or that chance child which was watching Lloyd and me, I remember pondering a twofold problem: first, whether, perhaps, a single bodily state had more advantages than ours possessed; and second, whether *all* other children were single. It occurs to me now that quite often problems puzzling me were twofold: possibly a trickle of Lloyd's cerebration penetrated my mind and one of the two linked problems was his.

When greedy Grandfather Ahem decided to show us to visitors for money, among the flocks that came there was always some eager rascal who wanted to hear us talk to each other. As happens with primitive minds, he demanded that his ears corroborate what his eyes saw. Our folks bullied us into gratifying such desires and could not understand what was so distressful about them. We could have pleaded shyness; but the truth was that we never really *spoke* to each other, even when we were alone, for the brief broken grunts of infrequent expostulation that we sometimes exchanged (when, for instance, one had just cut his foot and had had it bandaged and the other wanted to go paddling in the brook) could hardly pass for a dialogue. The communication of simple essential sensations we performed wordlessly: shed leaves riding the stream of our shared blood. Thin thoughts also managed to slip through and travel between us. Richer ones each kept to himself, but even then there occurred odd phenomena. This is why I suspect that despite his calmer nature, Lloyd was struggling with the same new realities that were puzzling me. He forgot much when he grew up. I have forgotten nothing.

Not only did our public expect us to talk, it also wanted us to play together. Dolts! They derived quite a kick from having us match wits at checkers or *muzla*. I suppose had we happened to be opposite-sex twins they would have made us commit incest in their presence. But since mutual games were no more customary with us than conversation, we suffered subtle torments when obliged to go through the cramped motions of bandying a ball somewhere between our breastbones or making believe to wrest a stick from each other. We drew wild applause by running around the yard with our arms around each other's shoulders. We could jump and whirl.

A salesman of patent medicine, a bald little fellow in a dirty-white Russian blouse, who knew some Turkish and English, taught us sentences in these languages; and then we had to demonstrate our ability to a fascinated audience. Their ardent faces still pursue me in my nightmares, for they come whenever my dream producer needs supers. I see again the gigantic bronze-faced shepherd in multi-colored rags, the soldiers from Karaz, the one-eyed hunch-backed Armenian tailor (a monster in his own right), the giggling girls, the sighing old women, the children, the young people in Western clothes—burning eyes, white teeth, black gaping mouths; and, of course, Grandfather Ahem, with his nose of yellow ivory and his beard of gray wool, directing the proceedings or counting the soiled paper money and wetting his big thumb. The linguist, he of the embroidered blouse and bald head, courted one of my aunts but kept watching Ahem enviously through his steel-rimmed spectacles.

By the age of nine, I knew quite clearly that Lloyd and I presented the rarest of freaks. This knowledge provoked in me neither any special elation nor any special shame; but once a hysterical cook, a mustached woman, who had taken a great liking to us and pitied our plight, declared with an atrocious oath that she would, then and there, slice us free by means of a shiny knife that she suddenly flourished (she was at once overpowered by our grandfather and one of our newly acquired uncles); and after that incident I would often dally with an indolent daydream, fancying myself somehow separated from poor Lloyd, who somehow retained his monsterhood.

I did not care for that knife business, and anyway the manner of separation remained very vague; but I distinctly imagined the sudden melting away of my shackles and the feeling of lightness and nakedness that would ensue. I imagined myself climbing over the fence—a fence with bleached skulls of farm animals that crowned its pickets—and descending toward the beach. I saw myself leaping from boulder to boulder and diving into the twinkling sea, and scrambling back onto the shore and scampering about with other naked children. I dreamed of this at night—saw myself fleeing from my grandfather and carrying away with me a toy, or a kitten, or a little crab pressed to my left side. I saw myself meeting poor Lloyd, who appeared to me in my dream hobbling along, hopelessly joined to a hobbling twin while I was free to dance around them and slap them on their humble backs.

I wonder if Lloyd had similar visions. It has been suggested by doctors that we sometimes pooled our minds when we dreamed. One gray-blue morning he picked up a twig and drew a ship with three masts in the dust. I had just seen myself drawing that ship in the dust of a dream I had dreamed the preceding night.

An ample black shepherd's cloak covered our shoulders, and, as we squatted on the ground, all but our heads and Lloyd's hand was concealed within its falling folds. The sun had just risen and the sharp March air was like layer upon layer of semitransparent ice through which the crooked Judas trees in rough bloom made blurry spots of purplish pink. The long low white house behind us, full of fat women and their foul-smelling husbands, was fast asleep. We did not say anything; we did not even look at each other; but, throwing his twig away, Lloyd put his right arm around my shoulder, as he always did when he wished both of us to walk fast; and with the edge of our common raiment trailing among dead weeds, while pebbles kept running from under our feet, we made our way toward the alley of cypresses that led down to the shore.

It was our first attempt to visit the sea that we could see from our hilltop softly glistening afar and leisurely, silently breaking on glossy rocks. I need not strain my memory at this point to place our stumbling flight at a definite turn in our destiny. A few weeks before, on our twelfth birthday, Grandfather Ibrahim had started to toy with the idea of sending us in the company of our newest uncle on a six-month tour through the country. They kept haggling about the terms, and had quarreled and even fought, Ahem getting the upper hand.

We feared our grandfather and loathed Uncle Novus. Presumably, after a dull forlorn fashion (knowing nothing of life, but being dimly aware that Uncle Novus was endeavoring to cheat Grandfather) we felt we should try to do something in order to prevent a showman from trundling us around in a moving prison, like apes or eagles; or perhaps we were prompted merely by the thought that this was our last chance to enjoy by ourselves our small freedom and do what we were absolutely forbidden to do: go beyond a certain picket fence, open a certain gate.

We had no trouble in opening that rickety gate, but did not manage to swing it back into its former position. A dirty-white lamb, with amber eyes and a carmine mark painted upon its hard flat forehead, followed us for a while before getting lost in the oak scrub. A little lower but still far above the valley, we had to cross the road that circled around the hill and connected our farm with the highway running along the shore. The thudding of hoofs and the rasping of wheels came descending upon us; and we dropped, cloak and all, behind a bush. When the rumble subsided, we crossed the road and continued along a weedy slope. The silvery sea gradually concealed itself behind cypresses and remnants of old stone walls. Our black cloak began to feel hot and heavy but still we persevered under its protection, being afraid that otherwise some passer-by might notice our infirmity.

We emerged upon the highway, a few feet from the audible sea—and there, waiting for us under a cypress, was a carriage we knew, a cartlike affair on high wheels, with Uncle Novus in the act of getting down from the box. Crafty, dark, ambitious, unprincipled little man! A few minutes before, he had caught sight of us from one of the galleries of our grandfather's house and had not been able to resist the temptation of taking advantage of an escapade which miraculously allowed him to seize us without any struggle or outcry. Swearing at the two timorous horses, he roughly helped us into the cart. He pushed our heads down and threatened to hurt us if we attempted to peep from under our cloak. Lloyd's arm was still around my shoulder, but a jerk of the cart shook it off. Now the wheels were crunching and rolling. It was some time before we realized that our driver was not taking us home.

Twenty years have passed since that gray spring morning, but it is much better preserved in my mind than many a later event. Again and again I run it before my eyes like a strip of cinematic film, as I have seen great jugglers do

174

when reviewing their acts. So I review all the stages and circumstances and incidental details of our abortive flight—the initial shiver, the gate, the lamb, the slippery slope under our clumsy feet. To the thrushes we flushed we must have presented an extraordinary sight, with that black cloak around us and our two shorn heads on thin necks sticking out of it. The heads turned this way and that, warily, as at last the shore-line highway was reached. If at that moment some adventurous stranger had stepped onto the shore from his boat in the bay, he would have surely experienced a thrill of ancient enchantment to find himself confronted by a gentle mythological monster in a landscape of cypresses and white stones. He would have worshiped it, he would have shed sweet tears. But, alas, there was nobody to greet us there save that worried crook, our nervous kidnaper, a small doll-faced man wearing cheap spectacles, one glass of which was doctored with a bit of tape.

Ithaca, 1950.

Mademoiselle O

1

I have often noticed that after I had bestowed on the characters of my novels some treasured item of my past, it would pine away in the artificial world where I had so abruptly placed it. Although it lingered on in my mind, its personal warmth, its retrospective appeal had gone and, presently, it became more closely identified with my novel than with my former self, where it had seemed to be so safe from the intrusion of the artist. Houses have crumbled in my memory as soundlessly as they did in the mute films of yore; and the portrait of my old French governess, whom I once lent to a boy in one of my books, is fading fast, now that it is engulfed in the description of a childhood entirely unrelated to my own. The man in me revolts against the fictionist and here is my desperate attempt to save what is left of poor Mademoiselle.

A large woman, a very stout woman, Mademoiselle rolled into our existence in 1905 when I was six and my brother five. There she is. I see so plainly her abundant dark hair, brushed up high and covertly graying; the three wrinkles on her austere forehead; her beetling brows; the steely eyes behind the black-rimmed pince-nez; that vestigial mustache; that blotchy complexion, which in moments of wrath develops an additional flush in the region of the third, and amplest, chin so regally spread over the frilled mountain of her blouse. And now she sits down, or rather she tackles the job of sitting down, the jelly of her jowl quaking, her prodigious posterior, with the three buttons on the side, lowering itself warily; then, at the last second, she surrenders her bulk to the wicker armchair, which out of sheer fright bursts into a salvo of crackling.

The winter she came was the only one of my childhood that I spent in the country. It was a year of strikes, riots, and police-inspired massacres; and I suppose my father wished to tuck his family away from the city, in our quiet country place, where his popularity with the peasants might mitigate, as he correctly surmised, the risk of agrarian troubles. It was also a particularly severe winter, producing as much snow as Mademoiselle might have expected to find in the Hyperborean gloom of remote Muscovy. When she alighted at the little station, from which she still had to travel half-a-dozen miles by sleigh to our country home, I was not there to greet her; but I do so now as I try to imagine what she saw and felt at that last stage of her fabulous and ill-timed journey. Her Russian vocabulary consisted, I know, of one short word, the same solitary word that years later she was to take back to Switzerland, where she had been born of French parents. This word, which in her pronunciation may be phonetically rendered as "giddy-eh," (actually it is *gde*

with *e* as in "yet") meant "Where?" And that was a good
deal. Uttered by her like the raucous cry of some lost bird,
it accumulated such interrogatory force that it sufficed for
all her needs. "Giddy-eh? Giddy-eh?" she would wail, not
only to find out her whereabouts but also to express an
abyss of misery: the fact that she was a stranger, ship-
wrecked, penniless, ailing, in search of the blessed land
where at last she would be understood.

I can visualize her, by proxy, as she stands in the middle
of the station platform, where she has just alighted, and
vainly my ghostly envoy offers her an arm that she cannot
see. The door of the waiting room opens with a shuddering
whine peculiar to nights of intense frost; a cloud of hot air
rushes out, almost as profuse as the steam from the great
stack of the panting engine; and now our coachman Zakhar
takes over—a burly man in sheepskin with the leather outside, his huge gloves protruding from his scarlet sash into
which he has stuffed them. I hear the snow crunching under
his felt boots while he busies himself with the luggage, the
jingling harness, and then his own nose, which he eases by
means of a dexterous flip of finger and thumb as he trudges
back round the sleigh. Slowly, with grim misgivings, Mademoiselle climbs in, clutching at her helper in mortal fear lest
the sleigh move off before her vast form is securely encased.
Finally, she settles down with a grunt and thrusts her fists
into her skimpy plush muff. At the juicy smack of their
driver's lips the horses strain their quarters, shift hoofs,
strain again; and then Mademoiselle gives a backward jerk
of her torso as the heavy sleigh is wrenched out of its world
of steel, fur, flesh, to enter a frictionless medium where it
skims along a spectral road that it seems barely to touch.

For one moment, thanks to the sudden radiance of a lone
lamp where the station square ends, a grossly exaggerated

shadow, also holding a muff, races beside the sleigh, climbs a billow of snow, and is gone, leaving Mademoiselle to be swallowed up by what she will later allude to, with awe and gusto, as "*le steppe*." There, in the limitless gloom, the changeable twinkle of remote village lights seems to her to be the yellow eyes of wolves. She is cold, she is frozen stiff, frozen "to the center of her brain," for she soars with the wildest hyperbole when not clinging to the safest old saw. Every now and then, she looks back to make sure that a second sleigh, bearing her trunk and hatbox, is following— always at the same distance, like those companionable phantoms of ships in polar waters which explorers have described. And let me not leave out the moon—for surely there must be a moon, the full, incredibly clear disc that goes so well with Russian lusty frosts. So there it comes, steering out of a flock of small dappled clouds, which it tinges with a vague iridescence; and, as it sails higher, it glazes the runner tracks left on the road, where every sparkling lump of snow is emphasized by a swollen shadow.

Very lovely, very lonesome. But what am I doing there in that stereoscopic dreamland? Somehow those two sleighs have slipped away; they have left my imaginary double behind on the blue-white road. No, even the vibration in my ears is not their receding bells, but my own blood singing. All is still, spellbound, enthralled by that great heavenly *O* shining above the Russian wilderness of my past. The snow is real, though, and as I bend to it and scoop up a handful, forty-five years crumble to glittering frost-dust between my fingers.

2

A kerosene lamp is steered into the gloaming. Gently it

floats and comes down; the hand of memory, now in a foot-
man's white cotton glove, places it in the center of a round
table. The flame is nicely adjusted, and a rosy, silk-flounced
lamp shade crowns the light. Revealed: a warm, bright
room in a snow-muffled house—soon to be termed *le château*
—built by my great-grandfather, who, being afraid of fires,
had the stair-case made of iron, so that when the house did
get burnt to the ground, sometime after the Soviet Revolution, those fretted steps remained standing there, all
alone but still leading up.

Some more about that room, please. The oval mirror.
Hanging on taut cords, its pure brow inclined, it strives
to retain the falling furniture and a slope of bright floor that
keep slipping from its embrace. The chandelier pendants.
These emit a delicate tinkling whenever anything is moved
in an upstairs room. Colored pencils. That tiny heap of
emerald pencil dust on the oilcloth where a penknife has
just done its recurrent duty. We are sitting at the table, my
brother and I and Miss Robinson, who now and then looks
at her watch: roads must be dreadful with all that snow; and
anyway many professional hardships lie in wait for the
vague French person who will replace her.

Now the colored pencils in more detail. The green one, by
a mere whirl of the wrist, could be made to produce a ruffled
tree, or the chimney smoke of a house where spinach was
cooking. The blue one drew a simple line across the page—
and the horizon of all seas was there. A nondescript blunt
one kept getting into one's way. The brown one was always
broken, and so was the red, but sometimes, just after it had
snapped, one could still make it serve by holding it so that
the loose tip was propped, none too securely, by a jutting
splinter. The little purple fellow, a special favorite of mine,
had got worn down so short as to become scarcely manage-

able. The white one alone, that lanky albino among pencils, kept its original length, or at least did so until I discovered that, far from being a fraud leaving no mark on the page, it was the ideal tool since I could imagine whatever I wished while I scrawled.

Alas, these pencils, too, have been distributed among the characters in my books to keep fictitious children busy; they are not quite my own now. Somewhere, in the apartment house of a chapter, in the hired room of a paragraph, I have also placed that tilted mirror, and the lamp, and the chandelier-drops. Few things are left, many have been squandered. Have I given away Box (son and husband of Loulou, the housekeeper's pet), that old brown dachshund fast asleep on the sofa? No, I think he is still mine. His grizzled muzzle, with the wart at the puckered corner of the mouth, is tucked into the curve of his hock, and from time to time a deep sigh distends his ribs. He is so old and his sleep is so thickly padded with dreams (about chewable slippers and a few last smells) that he does not stir when faint bells jingle outside. Then a pneumatic door heaves and clangs in the vestibule. She has come after all: I had so hoped she would not.

3

Another dog, the sweet-tempered sire of a ferocious family, a Great Dane not allowed in the house, played a pleasant part in an adventure that took place on one of the following days, if not the very day after. It so happened that my brother and I were left completely in charge of the newcomer. As I reconstruct it now, my mother had probably gone for a few hours to St. Petersburg (a distance of some fifty miles) where my father was deeply involved in the grave political events of that winter. She was pregnant and very nervous. Miss Robinson instead of staying to break in Mademoiselle had gone too—or perhaps my little sister, aged three, had inherited her. In order to prove that this was no way of treating us, I immediately formed the project of repeating the exciting performance of a year before, when we escaped from poor Miss Hunt in gay, populous Wiesbaden, a paradise of multicolored dead leaves. This time the countryside all around was a wilderness of snow, and it is hard to imagine what exactly could have been the goal of the journey I planned. We had just returned from our first afternoon walk with Mademoiselle and were throbbing with frustration and hatred. To keep up with an unfamiliar tongue (all we knew in the way of French were a few household words), and on top of it to be crossed in all our fond habits, was more than we could bear. The *bonne promenade* she had promised us had turned out to be a tedious stroll around the house where the snow had been cleared and the icy ground sprinkled with sand. She had had us wear things we never used to wear, even on the frostiest day—horrible gaiters and hoods that hampered our every movement. She had restrained us when we were tempted to explore the creamy, smooth swellings of snow that had been flower beds in summer. She had not allowed us to walk under the organ-pipelike system of huge icicles that hung from the eaves and gloriously burned in the low sun. As soon as we came back from that walk, we left Mademoiselle puffing on the steps of the vestibule and dashed indoors, giving her the impression that we were about to conceal ourselves in some remote room. Actually, we trotted on till we reached the other side of the house, and then, through a veranda, emerged into the garden again. The above-mentioned Great Dane was in the act of fussily adjusting himself to a nearby snowdrift, but while deciding which hind leg to lift he noticed us and at once joined us at a joyful gallop.

The three of us followed a fairly easy trail and, after plodding through deeper snow, reached the road that led to the village. Meanwhile the sun had set. Dusk came with uncanny suddenness. My brother declared he was cold and tired, but I urged him on and finally made him ride the dog (the only member of the party to be still enjoying himself). We had gone more than two miles and the moon was fantastically shiny, and my brother, in perfect silence, had begun to fall every now and then from his mount, when a servant with a lantern overtook us and led us home. "Giddy-eh, giddy-eh?" Mademoiselle was frantically shouting from the porch. I brushed past her without a word. My brother burst into tears, and gave himself up. The Great Dane, whose name was Turka, returned to his interrupted affairs in connection with serviceable and informative snowdrifts around the house.

4

In our childhood we know a lot about hands since they live and hover at the level of our stature; Mademoiselle's were unpleasant because of the froggy gloss on their tight skin besprinkled with brown ecchymotic spots. Before her time no stranger had ever stroked my face. Mademoiselle, as soon as she came, had taken me completely aback by patting my cheek in sign of spontaneous affection. All her mannerisms come back to me when I think of her hands. Her trick of peeling rather than sharpening a pencil, the point held toward her stupendous and sterile bosom swathed in green wool. The way she had of inserting her little finger into her ear and vibrating it very rapidly. The ritual observed every time she gave me a fresh copybook. Always panting a little, her mouth slightly open and emitting in quick succession a series of asthmatic puffs, she would open the copybook to make a margin in it; that is, she would sharply imprint a vertical line with her thumbnail, fold in the edge of the page, press, release, smooth it out with the heel of her hand, after which the book would be briskly twisted around and placed before me ready for use. A new pen followed; she would moisten the glistening nib with susurrus lips before dipping it into the baptismal ink font. Then, delighting in every limb of every limpid letter (especially so because the preceding copybook had ended in utter sloppiness), with exquisite care I would inscribe the word *Dictée* while Mademoiselle hunted through her collection of spelling tests for a good, hard passage.

5

Meanwhile the setting has changed. Hoarfrost and snow have been removed by a silent property man. The summer afternoon is alive with steep clouds breasting the blue. Eyed shadows move on the garden paths. Presently, lessons are over and Mademoiselle is reading to us on the veranda where the mats and plaited chairs develop a spicy, biscuity smell in the heat. On the white window sills, on the long window seats covered with faded calico, the sun breaks into geometrical gems after passing through rhomboids and squares of stained glass. This is the time when Mademoiselle is at her very best.

What a number of volumes she read through to us on that veranda! Her slender voice sped on and on, never weakening, without the slightest hitch or hesitation, an admirable reading machine wholly independent of her sick bronchial tubes. We got it all: *Les Malheurs de Sophie, Le Tour du Monde en Quatre-Vingts Jours, Le Petit Chose, Les Misérables, Le Comte de Monte Cristo,* many others. There she sat, distilling her reading voice from the still prison of her person. Apart from the lips, one of her chins, the smallest but true one, was the only mobile detail of her Buddha-like bulk. The black-rimmed pince-nez reflected eternity. Occasionally a fly would settle on her stern forehead and its three wrinkles would instantly leap up all together like three runners over three hurdles. But nothing whatever changed in the expression of her face—the face I so often tried to depict in my sketchbook, for its impassive and simple symmetry offered a far greater temptation to my stealthy pencil than the bowl of flowers or the decoy duck on the table before me, which I was supposedly drawing.

Presently my attention would wander still farther, and it was then, perhaps, that the rare purity of her rhythmic voice accomplished its true purpose. I looked at a cloud and years later was able to visualize its exact shape. The gardener was pottering among the peonies. A wagtail took a few steps, stopped as if it had remembered something—and then walked on, enacting its name. Coming from nowhere, a comma butterfly settled on the threshold, basked in the sun with its angular fulvous wings spread, suddenly closed them just to show the tiny initial chalked on their underside, and as suddenly darted away. But the most constant source of enchantment during those readings came from the harlequin pattern of colored panes inset in a whitewashed framework on either side of the veranda. The garden when viewed through these magic glasses grew strangely still and aloof. If one looked through blue glass, the sand turned to cinders while inky trees swam in a tropical sky. The yellow created an amber world infused with an extra strong brew of sunshine. The red made the foliage drip ruby dark upon a coral-tinted footpath. The green soaked greenery in a greener green. And when, after such richness, one turned to a small square of normal, savorless glass, with its lone mosquito or lame daddy longlegs, it was like taking a draught of water when one is not thirsty, and one saw a matter-of-fact white bench under familiar trees. But of all the windows this is the pane through which in later years parched nostalgia longed to peer.

Mademoiselle never found out how potent had been the even flow of her voice. The subsequent claims she put forward were quite different. "Ah," she sighed, "*comme on s'aimait*—didn't we love each other! Those good old days in the *château!* The dead wax doll we once buried under the oak! (No—a wool-stuffed Golliwogg.) And that time you and Serge ran away and left me stumbling and howling in the depths of the forest! (Exaggerated.) *Ah, la fessée que je vous ai flanquée*— My, what a spanking I gave you! (She did try to slap me once but the attempt was never repeated.) *Votre tante, la Princesse*, whom you struck with your little fist because she had been rude to me! (Do not remember.) And the way you whispered to me your childish troubles! (Never!) And the cozy nook in my room where you loved to snuggle because you felt so warm and secure!"

Mademoiselle's room, both in the country and in town, was a weird place to me—a kind of hothouse sheltering a thick-leaved plant imbued with a heavy, queerly acrid odor. Although next to ours, when we were small, it did not seem to belong to our pleasant, well-aired home. In that sickening mist, reeking, among other effluvia, of the brown smell of oxidized apple peel, the lamp burned low, and strange objects glimmered upon the writing desk: a lacquered box with licorice sticks, black segments of which she would hack off with her penknife and put to melt under her tongue; a picture postcard of a lake and a castle with mother-of-pearl spangles for windows; a bumpy ball of tightly rolled bits of silver paper that came from all those chocolates she used to consume at night; photographs of the nephew who had died, of his mother who had signed her picture *Mater Dolorosa,* and of a certain Monsieur de Marante who had been forced by his family to marry a rich widow.

Lording it over the rest was one in a noble frame incrusted with garnets; it showed, in three-quarter view, a slim young brunette clad in a close-fitting dress, with brave eyes and abundant hair. "A braid as thick as my arm and reaching down to my ankles!" was Mademoiselle's melodramatic comment. For this had been she—but in vain did my eyes probe her familiar form to try and extract the graceful creature it had engulfed. Such discoveries as my awed brother and I did make merely increased the difficulties of that task; and the grownups who during the day beheld a densely clothed Mademoiselle never saw what we children saw when, roused from her sleep by one of us shrieking himself out of a bad dream, disheveled, candle in hand, a gleam of gilt lace on the blood-red dressing gown that could not quite wrap her quaking mass, the ghastly Jézabel of Racine's absurd play stomped barefooted into our bedroom.

All my life I have been a poor go-to-sleeper. No matter how great my weariness, the wrench of parting with consciousness is unspeakably repulsive to me. I loathe Somnus, that black-masked headsman binding me to the block; and if in the course of years I have got so used to my nightly ordeal as almost to swagger while the familiar ax is coming out of its great velvet-lined case, initially I had no such comfort or defense: I had nothing—save a door left slightly ajar into Mademoiselle's room. Its vertical line of meek light was something I could cling to, since in absolute darkness my head would swim, just as the soul dissolves in the blackness of sleep.

Saturday night used to be a pleasurable prospect because that was the night Mademoiselle indulged in the luxury of a weekly bath, thus granting a longer lease to my tenuous gleam. But then a subtler torture set in. The nursery bathroom in our St. Petersburg house was at the end of a Z-shaped corridor some twenty heartbeats' distance from my bed, and between dreading Mademoiselle's return from the bathroom to her lighted bedroom and envying my brother's stolid snore, I could never really put my additional time to profit by deftly getting to sleep while a chink in the dark still bespoke a speck of myself in nothingness. At length they would come, those inexorable steps, plodding along the passage and causing some little glass object, which had been secretly sharing my vigil, to tinkle in dismay on its shelf.

Now she has entered her room. A brisk interchange of light values tells me that the candle on her bed table takes over the job of the lamp on her desk. My line of light is still there, but it has grown old and wan, and flickers whenever Mademoiselle makes her bed creak by moving. For I still hear her. Now it is a silvery rustle spelling "Suchard"; now the trk-trk-trk of a fruit knife cutting the pages of *La Revue des Deux Mondes*. I hear her panting slightly. And all the time I am in acute distress, desperately trying to coax sleep, opening my eyes every few seconds to check the faded gleam, and imagining paradise as a place where a sleepless neighbor reads an endless book by the light of an eternal candle.

The inevitable happens: the pince-nez case shuts with a snap, the review shuffles onto the marble of the bed table, and gustily Mademoiselle's pursed lips blow; the first attempt fails, a groggy flame squirms and ducks; then comes a second lunge, and light collapses. In that pitchy blackness I lose my bearings, my bed seems to be slowly drifting, panic makes me sit up and stare; finally my dark-adapted eyes sift out, among entoptic floaters, certain more precious blurrings that roam in aimless amnesia until, half-remembering, they settle down as the dim folds of window curtains behind which street lights are remotely alive.

How utterly foreign to the troubles of the night were those exciting St. Petersburg mornings when the fierce and tender, damp and dazzling arctic spring bundled away broken ice down the sea-bright Neva! It made the roofs shine. It painted the slush in the streets a rich purplish-blue shade which I have never seen anywhere since. Mademoiselle, her coat of imitation seal majestically swelling on her bosom, sat in the back seat of the landau with my brother next to her and me facing them—joined to them by the valley of the lap rug; and as I looked up I could see, strung on ropes from house front to house front high above the street, great, tensely smooth, semitransparent banners billowing, their three wide bands—pale red, pale blue, and merely pale—deprived by the sun and the flying cloud shadows of any too blunt connection with a national holiday, but undoubtedly celebrating now, in the city of memory, the essence of that spring day, the swish of the mud, the ruffled exotic bird with one bloodshot eye on Mademoiselle's hat.

6

She spent seven years with us, lessons getting rarer and rarer and her temper worse and worse. Still, she seemed like a rock of grim permanence when compared to the ebb and flow of English governesses and Russian tutors passing through our large household. She was on bad terms with all of them. Seldom less than a dozen people sat down for meals and when, on birthdays, this number rose to thirty or more, the question of place at table became a particularly burning one for Mademoiselle. Uncles and aunts and cousins would arrive on such days from neighboring estates, and the village doctor would come in his dogcart, and the village schoolmaster would be heard blowing his nose in the cool hall, where he passed from mirror to mirror with a greenish, damp, creaking bouquet of lilies of the valley or a sky-colored, brittle one of cornflowers in his fist.

If Mademoiselle found herself seated too far at the end of the table, and especially if she lost precedence to a certain poor relative who was almost as fat as she (*"Je suis une sylphide à côté d'elle,"* Mademoiselle would say with a shrug of contempt), then her sense of injury caused her lips to twitch in a would-be ironical smile—and when a naïve neighbor would smile back, she would rapidly shake her head, as if coming out of some very deep meditation, with the remark: *"Excusez-moi, je souriais à mes tristes pensées."*

And as though nature had not wished to spare her anything that makes one supersensitive, she was hard of hearing. Sometimes at table we boys would suddenly become aware of two big tears crawling down Mademoiselle's ample cheeks. "Don't mind me," she would say in a small

191

voice, and she kept on eating till the unwiped tears blinded her; then, with a heartbroken hiccup she would rise and blunder out of the dining room. Little by little the truth would come out. The general talk had turned, say, on the subject of the warship my uncle commanded, and she had perceived in this a sly dig at her Switzerland that had no navy. Or else it was because she fancied that whenever French was spoken, the game consisted in deliberately preventing her from directing and bejeweling the conversation. Poor lady, she was always in such a nervous hurry to seize control of intelligible table talk before it bolted back into Russian that no wonder she bungled her cue.

"And your Parliament, Sir, how is it getting along?" she would suddenly burst out brightly from her end of the table, challenging my father, who, after a harassing day, was not exactly eager to discuss troubles of the State with a singularly unreal person who neither knew nor cared anything about them. Thinking that someone had referred to music, "But Silence, too, may be beautiful," she would bubble. "Why, one evening, in a desolate valley of the Alps, I actually *heard* Silence." Sallies like these, especially when growing deafness led her to answer questions none had put, resulted in a painful hush, instead of touching off the rockets of a sprightly *causerie*.

And, really, her French was so lovely! Ought one to have minded the shallowness of her culture, the bitterness of her temper, the banality of her mind, when that pearly language of hers purled and scintillated, as innocent of sense as the alliterative sins of Racine's pious verse? My father's library, not her limited lore, taught me to appreciate authentic poetry; nevertheless, something of her tongue's limpidity and luster has had a singularly bracing effect upon me, like those sparkling salts that are used to purify the blood. This is why it makes me so sad to imagine now the anguish Mademoiselle must have felt at seeing how lost, how little valued was the nightingale voice which came from her elephantine body. She stayed with us long, much too long, obstinately hoping for some miracle that would transform her into a kind of Madame de Rambouillet holding a gilt-and-satin *salon* of poets, princes, and statesmen under her brilliant spell.

She would have gone on hoping had it not been for one Lenski, a young Russian tutor, with mild myopic eyes and strong political opinions, who had been engaged to coach us in various subjects and participate in our sports. He had had several predecessors, none of whom Mademoiselle had liked, but he, as she put it, was "*le comble.*" While venerating my father, Lenski could not quite stomach certain aspects of our household, such as footmen and French, which last he considered an aristocratic convention of no use in a liberal's home. On the other hand, Mademoiselle decided that if Lenski answered her point-blank questions only with short grunts (which he tried to Germanize for want of a better language) it was not because he could not understand French, but because he wished to insult her in front of everybody.

I can hear and see Mademoiselle requesting him in dulcet tones, but with an ominous quiver of her upper lip, to pass her the bread; and, likewise, I can hear and see Lenski Frenchlessly and unflinchingly going on with his soup; finally, with a slashing "*Pardon, Monsieur,*" Mademoiselle would swoop right across his plate, snatch up the breadbasket, and recoil again with a "*Merci!*" so charged with irony that Lenski's downy ears would turn the hue of geraniums. "The brute! The cad! The Nihilist!" she would sob later in her room—which was no longer next to ours though still on the same floor.

If Lenski happened to come tripping downstairs while, with an asthmatic pause every ten steps or so, she was working her way up (for the little hydraulic elevator of our house in St. Petersburg would constantly, and rather insultingly, refuse to function), Mademoiselle maintained that he had viciously bumped into her, pushed her, knocked her down, and we already could see him trampling her prostrate body. More and more frequently she would leave the table, and the dessert she would have missed was diplomatically sent up in her wake. From her remote room she would write a sixteen-page letter to my mother, who, upon hurrying upstairs, would find her dramatically packing her trunk. And then, one day, she was allowed to go on with her packing.

7

She returned to Switzerland. World War I came, then the Revolution. In the early twenties, long after our correspondence had fizzled out, by a fluke move of life in exile I chanced to visit Lausanne with a college friend of mine, so I thought I might as well look up Mademoiselle, if she were still alive.

She was. Stouter than ever, quite gray and almost totally deaf, she welcomed me with a tumultuous outburst of affection. Instead of the Château de Chillon picture, there was now one of a garish troika. She spoke as warmly of her life in Russia as if it were her own lost homeland. Indeed, I found in the neighborhood quite a colony of such old Swiss governesses. Clustering together in a constant seething of competitive reminiscences, they formed a small island in an environment that had grown alien to them. Mademoiselle's bosom friend was now mummylike Mlle. Golay, my mother's former governess, still prim and pessimistic at eighty-five; she had remained in our family long after my mother had married, and her return to Switzerland had preceded only by a couple of years that of Mademoiselle, with whom she had not been on speaking terms when both had been living under our roof. One is always at home in one's past, which partly explains those pathetic ladies' posthumous love for another country, which they never had really known and in which none of them had been very content.

As no conversation was possible because of Mademoiselle's deafness, my friend and I decided to bring her next day the appliance which we gathered she could not afford. She adjusted the clumsy thing improperly at first, but no sooner had she done so than she turned to me with a dazzled look of moist wonder and bliss in her eyes. She swore she could hear every word, every murmur of mine. She could not for, having my doubts, I had not spoken. If I had, I would have told her to thank my friend, who had paid for the instrument. Was it, then, silence she heard, that Alpine Silence she had talked about in the past? In that past, she had been lying to herself; now she was lying to me.

Before leaving for Basle and Berlin, I happened to be walking along the lake in the cold, misty night. At one spot a lone light dimly diluted the darkness. In its nimbus the mist seemed transformed into a visible drizzle. "*Il pleut toujours en Suisse*" was one of those casual comments which, formerly, had made Mademoiselle weep. Below, a wide ripple, almost a wave, and something vaguely white attracted my eye. As I came quite close to the lapping water, I saw what it was—an aged swan, a large, uncouth, dodolike creature, making ridiculous efforts to hoist himself into a moored boat. He could not do it. The heavy, impotent flapping of his wings, their slippery sound against the rocking and plashing boat, the gluey glistening of the dark swell where it caught the light—all seemed for a moment laden with that strange significance which sometimes in dreams is attached to a finger pressed to mute lips and then pointed at something the dreamer has no time to distinguish before waking with a start. But although I soon forgot that dismal night, it was, oddly enough, that night, that compound image—shudder and swan and swell—which first came to my mind when a couple of years later I learned that Mademoiselle had died.

She had spent all her life in feeling miserable; this misery was her native element; its fluctuations, its varying depths, alone gave her the impression of moving and living. What bothers me is that a sense of misery, and nothing else, is not enough to make a permanent soul. My enormous and morose Mademoiselle is all right on earth but impossible in eternity. Have I really salvaged her from fiction? Just before the rhythm I hear falters and fades, I catch myself wondering whether, during the years I knew her, I had not kept utterly missing something in her that was far more she than her chins or her ways or even her French—something perhaps akin to that last glimpse of her, to the radiant deceit she had used in order to have me depart pleased with my own kindness, or to that swan whose agony was so much closer to artistic truth than a drooping dancer's pale arms; something, in short, that I could appreciate only after the things and beings that I had most loved in the security of my childhood had been turned to ashes or shot through the heart.

Paris, 1939.

Lance

1

The name of the planet, presuming it has already received one, is immaterial. At its most favorable opposition, it may very well be separated from the earth by only as many miles as there are years between last Friday and the rise of the Himalayas—a million times the reader's average age. In the telescopic field of one's fancy, through the prism of one's tears, any particularities it presents should be no more striking than those of existing planets. A rosy globe, marbled with dusky blotches, it is one of the countless objects diligently revolving in the infinite and gratuitous awfulness of fluid space.

My planet's *maria* (which are not seas) and its *lacus* (which are not lakes) have also, let us suppose, received names; some less jejune, perhaps, than those of garden roses; others, more pointless than the surnames of their observers (for, to take actual cases, that an astronomer should have been called Lampland is as marvelous as that an entomologist should have been called Krautwurm); but most of them of so antique a style as to vie in sonorous and corrupt enchantment with place names pertaining to romances of chivalry.

Just as our Pinedales, down here, have often little to offer beyond a shoe factory on one side of the tracks and the rusty inferno of an automobile dump on the other, so those seductive Arcadias and Icarias and Zephyrias on planetary maps may quite likely turn out to be dead deserts lacking even the milkweed that graces our dumps. Selenographers will confirm this, but then, their lenses serve them better than ours do. In the present instance, the greater the magnification, the more the mottling of the planet's surface looks as if it were seen by a submerged swimmer peering up through semitranslucent water. And if certain connected markings resemble in a shadowy way the line-and-hole pattern of a Chinese-checkers board, let us consider them geometrical hallucinations.

I not only debar a too definite planet from any role in my story—from the role every dot and full stop should play in my story (which I see as a kind of celestial chart)—I also refuse to have anything to do with those technical prophecies that scientists are reported to make to reporters. Not for me is the rocket racket. Not for me are the artificial little satellites that the earth is promised; landing starstrips for spaceships ("spacers")—one, two, three, four, and then thousands of strong castles in the air each complete with cookhouse and keep, set up by terrestrial nations in a frenzy of competitive confusion, phony gravitation, and savagely flapping flags.

Another thing I have not the slightest use for is the

special-equipment business—the airtight suit, the oxygen apparatus—suchlike contraptions. Like old Mr. Boke, of whom we shall hear in a minute, I am eminently qualified to dismiss these practical matters (which anyway are doomed to seem absurdly impractical to future spaceshipmen, such as old Boke's only son), since the emotions that gadgets provoke in me range from dull distrust to morbid trepidation. Only by a heroic effort can I make myself unscrew a bulb that has died an inexplicable death and screw in another, which will light up in my face with the hideous instancy of a dragon's egg hatching in one's bare hand.

Finally, I utterly spurn and reject so-called "science fiction." I have looked into it, and found it as boring as the mystery-story magazines—the same sort of dismally pedestrian writing with oodles of dialogue and loads of commutational humor. The clichés are, of course, disguised; essentially, they are the same throughout all cheap reading matter, whether it spans the universe or the living room. They are like those "assorted" cookies that differ from one another only in shape and shade, whereby their shrewd makers ensnare the salivating consumer in a mad Pavlovian world where, at no extra cost, variations in simple visual values influence and gradually replace flavor, which thus goes the way of talent and truth.

So the good guy grins, and the villain sneers, and a noble heart sports a slangy speech. Star tsars, directors of Galactic Unions, are practically replicas of those peppy, redhaired executives in earthy earth jobs, that illustrate with their little crinkles the human interest stories of the wellthumbed slicks in beauty parlors. Invaders of Denebola and Spica, Virgo's finest, bear names beginning with Mac; cold scientists are usually found under Steins; some of them share with the supergalactic gals such abstract labels as Biola or Vala. Inhabitants of foreign planets, "intelligent" beings, humanoid or of various mythic makes, have one remarkable trait in common: their intimate structure is never depicted. In a supreme concession to biped propriety, not only do centaurs wear loincloths; they wear them about their forelegs.

This seems to complete the elimination—unless anybody wants to discuss the question of time? Here again, in order to focalize young Emery L. Boke, that more or less remote descendant of mine who is to be a member of the first interplanetary expedition (which, after all, is the one humble postulate of my tale), I gladly leave the replacement by a pretentious "2" or "3" of the honest "1" in our "1900" to the capable paws of *Starzan* and other comics and atomics. Let it be 2145 A.D. or 200 A.A., it does not matter. I have no desire to barge into vested interests of any kind. This is strictly an amateur performance, with quite casual stage properties and a minimum of scenery, and the quilled remains of a dead porcupine in a corner of the old barn. We are here among friends, the Browns and the Bensons, the Whites and the Wilsons, and when somebody goes out for a smoke, he hears the crickets, and a distant farm dog (who waits, between barks, to listen to what we cannot hear). The summer night sky is a mess of stars. Emery Lancelot Boke, at twenty-one, knows immeasurably more about them than I, who am fifty and terrified.

2

Lance is tall and lean, with thick tendons and greenish veins on his sun-tanned forearms and a scar on his brow. When doing nothing—when sitting ill at ease as he sits now,

leaning forward from the edge of a low armchair, his
shoulders hunched up, his elbows propped on his big knees
—he has a way of slowly clasping and unclasping his handsome hands, a gesture I borrow for him from one of his
ancestors. An air of gravity, of uncomfortable concentra-
tion (all thought is uncomfortable, and young thought
especially so), is his usual expression; at the moment, however, it is a manner of mask, concealing his furious desire
to get rid of a long-drawn tension. As a rule, he does not
smile often, and besides "smile" is too smooth a word for
the abrupt, bright contortion that now suddenly illumes
his mouth and eyes as the shoulders hunch higher, the
moving hands stop in a clasped position and he lightly
stamps the toe of one foot. His parents are in the room, and
also a chance visitor, a fool and a bore, who is not aware of
what is happening—for this is an awkward moment in a
gloomy house on the eve of a fabulous departure.

An hour goes by. At last the visitor picks up his top hat
from the carpet and leaves. Lance remains alone with his
parents, which only serves to increase the tension. Mr.
Boke I see plainly enough. But I cannot visualize Mrs. Boke
with any degree of clarity, no matter how deep I sink into
my difficult trance. I know that her cheerfulness—small
talk, quick beat of eyelashes—is something she keeps up
not so much for the sake of her son as for that of her husband, and his aging heart, and old Boke realizes this only
too well and, on top of his own monstrous anguish, he has
to cope with her feigned levity, which disturbs him more
than would an utter and unconditional collapse. I am somewhat disappointed that I cannot make out her features.
All I manage to glimpse is an effect of melting light on one
side of her misty hair, and in this, I suspect, I am insidiously
influenced by the standard artistry of modern photography

and I feel how much easier writing must have been in former days when one's imagination was not hemmed in by innumerable visual aids, and a frontiersman looking at his first giant cactus or his first high snows was not necessarily reminded of a tire company's pictorial advertisement.

In the case of Mr. Boke, I find myself operating with the features of an old professor of history, a brilliant medievalist, whose white whiskers, pink pate, and black suit are famous on a certain sunny campus in the deep South, but whose sole asset in connection with this story (apart from a slight resemblance to a long-dead great-uncle of mine) is that his appearance is out of date. Now if one is perfectly honest with oneself, there is nothing extraordinary in the tendency to give to the manners and clothes of a distant day (which happens to be placed in the future) an old-fashioned tinge, a badly pressed, badly groomed, dusty something, since the terms "out of date," "not of our age," and so on are in the long run the only ones in which we are able to imagine and express a strangeness no amount of research can foresee. The future is but the obsolete in reverse.

In that shabby room, in the tawny lamplight, Lance talks of some last things. He has recently brought from a desolate spot in the Andes, where he has been climbing some as yet unnamed peak, a couple of adolescent chinchillas —cinder-gray, phenomenally furry, rabbit-sized rodents (*Hystricomorpha*), with long whiskers, round rumps, and petallike ears. He keeps them indoors in a wire-screened pen and gives them peanuts, puffed rice, raisins to eat, and, as a special treat, a violet or an aster. He hopes they will breed in the fall. He now repeats to his mother a few emphatic instructions—to keep his pets' food crisp and their pen dry, and never forget their daily dust bath (fine sand mixed with powdered chalk) in which they roll and kick most lustily. While this is being discussed, Mr. Boke lights and relights a pipe and finally puts it away. Every now and then, with a false air of benevolent absent-mindedness, the old man launches upon a series of sounds and motions that deceive nobody; he clears his throat and, with his hands behind his back, drifts towards a window; or he begins to produce a tight-lipped tuneless humming; and seemingly driven by that small nasal motor, he wanders out of the parlor. But no sooner has he left the stage than he throws off, with a dreadful shiver, the elaborate structure of his gentle, bumbling impersonation act. In a bedroom or bathroom, he stops as if to take, in abject solitude, a deep spasmodic draught from some secret flask, and presently staggers out again, drunk with grief.

The stage has not changed when he quietly returns to it, buttoning his coat and resuming that little hum. It is now a matter of minutes. Lance inspects the pen before he goes, and leaves Chin and Chilla sitting on their haunches, each holding a flower. The only other thing that I know about these last moments is that any such talk as "Sure you haven't forgotten the silk shirt that came from the wash?" or "You remember where you put those new slippers?" is excluded. Whatever Lance takes with him is already collected at the mysterious and unmentionable and absolutely awful place of his zero-hour departure; he needs nothing of what we need; and he steps out of the house, empty-handed and hatless, with the casual lightness of one walking to the newsstand—or to a glorious scaffold.

3

Terrestrial space loves concealment. The most it yields

to the eye is a panoramic view. The horizon closes upon the receding traveler like a trap door in slow motion. For those who remain, any town a day's journey from here is invisible, whereas you can easily see such transcendencies as, say, a lunar amphitheater and the shadow cast by its circular ridge. The conjurer who displays the firmament has rolled up his sleeves and performs in full view of the little spectators. Planets may dip out of sight (just as objects are obliterated by the blurry curve of one's own cheekbone); but they are back when the earth turns its head. The nakedness of the night is appalling. Lance has left; the fragility of his young limbs grows in direct ratio to the distance he covers. From their balcony, the old Bokes look at the infinitely perilous night sky and wildly envy the lot of fishermen's wives.

If Boke's sources are accurate, the name "Lanceloz del Lac" occurs for the first time in Verse 3676 of the twelfth-century "Roman de la Charrete." Lance, Lancelin, Lance-lotik—diminutives murmured at the brimming, salty, moist stars. Young knights in their teens learning to harp, hawk, and hunt; the Forest Dangerous and the Dolorous Tower; Aldebaran, Betelgeuze—the thunder of Saracenic war cries. Marvelous deeds of arms, marvelous warriors, sparkling within the awful constellations above the Bokes' balcony: Sir Percard the Black Knight, and Sir Perimones the Red Knight, and Sir Pertolepe the Green Knight, and Sir Persant the Indigo Knight, and that bluff old party Sir Grummore Grummursum, muttering northern oaths under his breath. The field glass is not much good, the chart is all crumpled and damp, and: "You do not hold the flashlight properly"—this to Mrs. Boke.

Draw a deep breath. Look again.

Lancelot is gone; the hope of seeing him in life is about

equal to the hope of seeing him in eternity. Lancelot is banished from the country of L'Eau Grise (as we might call the Great Lakes) and now rides up in the dust of the night sky almost as fast as our local universe (with the balcony and the pitch-black, optically spotted garden) speeds toward King Arthur's Harp, where Vega burns and beckons—one of the few objects that can be identified by the aid of this goddam diagram. The sidereal haze makes the Bokes dizzy—gray incense, insanity, infinity-sickness. But they cannot tear themselves away from the nightmare of space, cannot go back to the lighted bedroom, a corner of which shows in the glass door. And presently *the* planet rises, like a tiny bonfire.

There, to the right, is the Bridge of the Sword leading to the Otherworld (*"dont nus estranges ne retorne"*). Lancelot crawls over it in great pain, in ineffable anguish. "Thou shalt not pass a pass that is called the Pass Perilous." But another enchanter commands: "You shall. You shall even acquire a sense of humor that will tide you over the trying spots." The brave old Bokes think they can distinguish Lance scaling, on crampons, the verglased rock of the sky or silently breaking trail through the soft snows of nebulae. Boötes, somewhere between Camp X and XI, is a great glacier all rubble and icefall. We try to make out the serpentine route of ascent; seem to distinguish the light leanness of Lance among the several roped silhouettes. Gone! Was it he or Denny (a young biologist, Lance's best friend)? Waiting in the dark valley at the foot of the vertical sky, we recall (Mrs. Boke more clearly than her husband) those special names for crevasses and Gothic structures of ice that Lance used to mouth with such professional gusto in his alpine boyhood (he is several light-years older by now); the séracs and the schrunds; the avalanche and its thud; French echoes and Germanic magic hobnailnobbing up there as they do in medieval romances.

Ah, there he is again! Crossing through a notch between two stars; then, very slowly, attempting a traverse on a cliff face so sheer, and with such delicate holds that the mere evocation of those groping fingertips and scraping boots fills one with acrophobic nausea. And through streaming tears the old Bokes see Lance now marooned on a shelf of stone and now climbing again and now, dreadfully safe, with his ice ax and pack, on a peak above peaks, his eager profile rimmed with light.

Or is he already on his way down? I assume that no news comes from the explorers and that the Bokes prolong their pathetic vigils. As they wait for their son to return, his every avenue of descent seems to run into the precipice of their despair. But perhaps he has swung over those high-angled wet slabs that fall away vertically into the abyss, has mastered the overhang, and is now blissfully glissading down steep celestial snows?

As, however, the Bokes' doorbell does not ring at the logical culmination of an imagined series of footfalls (no matter how patiently we space them as they come nearer and nearer in our mind), we have to thrust him back and have him start his ascent all over again, and then put him even further back, so that he is still at headquarters (where the tents are, and the open latrines, and the begging, black-footed children) long after we had pictured him bending under the tulip tree to walk up the lawn to the door and the doorbell. As if tired by the many appearances he has made in his parents' minds, Lance now plows wearily through mud puddles, then up a hillside, in the haggard landscape of a distant war, slipping and scrambling up the dead grass of the slope. There is some routine rock work ahead, and then the summit. The ridge is won. Our losses are heavy. How is one notified? By wire? By registered letter? And who is the executioner—a special messenger or the regular plodding, florid-nosed postman, always a little high (he has troubles of his own)? Sign here. Big thumb. Small cross. Weak pencil. Its dull-violet wood. Return it. The illegible signature of teetering disaster.

But nothing comes. A month passes. Chin and Chilla are in fine shape and seem very fond of each other—sleep together in the nest box, cuddled up in a fluffy ball. After many tries, Lance had discovered a sound with definite chinchillan appeal, produced by pursing the lips and emitting in rapid succession several soft, moist "surpths," as if taking sips from a straw when most of one's drink is finished and only its dregs are drained. But his parents cannot produce it—the pitch is wrong or something. And there is such an intolerable silence in Lance's room, with its battered books, and the spotty white shelves, and the old shoes, and the relatively new tennis racket in its preposterously secure press, and a penny on the closet floor—and all this begins to undergo a prismatic dissolution, but then you tighten the screw and everything is again in focus. And presently the Bokes return to their balcony. Has he reached his goal—and if so, does he see us?

4

The classical ex-mortal leans on his elbow from a flowered ledge to contemplate this earth, this toy, this teetotum gyrating on slow display in its model firmament, every feature so gay and clear—the painted oceans, and the praying woman of the Baltic, and a still of the elegant Americas caught in their trapeze act, and Australia like a baby Africa lying on its side. There may be people among my coevals who half expect their spirits to look down from Heaven with a shudder and a sigh at their native planet and see it girdled with latitudes, stayed with meridians, and marked, perhaps, with the fat, black, diabolically curving arrows of global wars; or, more pleasantly, spread out before their gaze like one of those picture maps of vacational Eldorados, with a reservation Indian beating a drum here, a girl clad in shorts there, conical conifers climbing the cones of mountains, and anglers all over the place.

Actually, I suppose, my young descendant on his first night out, in the imagined silence of an inimaginable world, would have to view the surface features of our globe through the depth of its atmosphere; this would mean dust, scattered reflections, haze, and all kinds of optical pitfalls, so that continents, if they appeared at all through the varying clouds, would slip by in queer disguises, with inexplicable gleams of color and unrecognizable outlines.

But all this is a minor point. The main problem is: Will the mind of the explorer survive the shock? One tries to perceive the nature of that shock as plainly as mental safety permits. And if the mere act of imagining the matter is fraught with hideous risks, how, then, will the real pang be endured and overcome?

First of all, Lance will have to deal with the atavistic moment. Myths have become so firmly entrenched in the radiant sky that common sense is apt to shirk the task of getting at the uncommon sense behind them. Immortality must have a star to stand on if it wishes to branch and blossom and support thousands of blue-plumed angel birds all singing as sweetly as little eunuchs. Deep in the human mind, the concept of dying is synonymous with that of leaving the earth. To escape its gravity means to transcend the grave, and a man upon finding himself on another planet has really no way of proving to himself that he is not dead— that the naïve old myth has not come true.

I am not concerned with the moron, the ordinary hairless ape, who takes everything in his stride; his only childhood memory is of a mule that bit him; his only consciousness of the future a vision of board and bed. What I am thinking of is the man of imagination and science, whose courage is infinite because his curiosity surpasses his courage. Nothing will keep him back. He is the ancient *curieux*, but of a hardier build, with a ruddier heart. When it comes to exploring a celestial body, his is the satisfaction of a passionate desire to feel with his own fingers, to stroke, and inspect, and smile at, and inhale, and stroke again—with that same smile of nameless, moaning, melting pleasure— the never-before-touched matter of which the celestial object is made. Any true scientist (not, of course, the fraudulent mediocrity, whose only treasure is the ignorance he hides like a bone) should be capable of experiencing that sensuous pleasure of direct and divine knowledge. He may be twenty and he may be eighty-five but without that tingle there is no science. And of that stuff Lance is made.

Straining my fancy to the utmost, I see him surmounting the panic that the ape might not experience at all. No doubt Lance may have landed in an orange-colored dust cloud somewhere in the middle of the Tharsis desert (if it is a desert) or near some purple pool—Phoenicis or Oti (if these are lakes after all). But on the other hand . . . You see, as things go in such matters, something is sure to be solved at once, terribly and irrevocably, while other things come up one by one and are puzzled out gradually. When I was a boy . . .

When I was a boy of seven or eight, I used to dream a vaguely recurrent dream set in a certain environment, which I have never been able to recognize and identify in any rational manner, though I have seen many strange lands. I am inclined to make it serve now, in order to patch up a gaping hole, a raw wound in my story. There was nothing spectacular about that environment, nothing monstrous or even odd: just a bit of noncommittal stability represented by a bit of level ground and filmed over with a bit of neutral nebulosity; in other words, the indifferent back of a view rather than its face. —the nuisance of that dream was that for some reason I could not walk *around* the view to meet it on equal terms. There lurked in the mist a mass of something—mineral matter or the like—oppressively and quite meaninglessly shaped, and, in the course of my dream, I kept filling some kind of receptacle (translated as "pail") with smaller shapes (translated as "pebbles"), and my nose was bleeding but I was too impatient and excited to do anything about it. And every time I had that dream, suddenly somebody would start screaming behind me, and I awoke screaming too, thus prolonging the initial anonymous shriek, with its initial note of rising exultation, but with no meaning attached to it any more—if there *had* been a meaning. Speaking of Lance, I would like to submit that something on the lines of my dream— But the funny thing is that as I reread what I have set down, its background, the factual memory vanishes—has vanished altogether by now—and I have no means of proving to myself that there is any personal experience behind its description. What I wanted to say was that perhaps Lance and his companions, when they reached their planet, felt something akin to my dream—which is no longer mine.

5

And they were back! A horseman, clappity-clap, gallops up the cobbled street to the Bokes' house through the driving rain and shouts out the tremendous news as he stops short at the gate, near the dripping liriodendron, while the Bokes come tearing out of the house like two hystricomorphic rodents. They are back! The pilots, and the astrophysicists, and one of the naturalists, are back (the other, Denny, is dead and has been left in Heaven, the old myth scoring a curious point there).

On the sixth floor of a provincial hospital, carefully hidden from newspapermen, Mr. and Mrs. Boke are told that their boy is in a little waiting room, second to the right, ready to receive them; there is something, a kind of hushed deference, about the tone of this information, as if it referred to a fairy tale king. They will enter quietly; a nurse, a Mrs. Coover, will be there all the time. Oh, he's all right, they are told—can go home next week, as a matter of fact. However, they should not stay more than a couple of minutes, and no questions, please—just chat about something or other. *You* know. And then say you will be coming again tomorrow or day after tomorrow.

Lance, gray-robed, crop-haired, tan gone, changed, unchanged, changed, thin, nostrils stopped with absorbent cotton, sits on the edge of a couch, his hands clasped, a little embarrassed. Gets up wavily, with a beaming grimace, and sits down again. Mrs. Coover, the nurse, has blue eyes and no chin.

A ripe silence. Then Lance: "It was wonderful. Perfectly wonderful. I am going back in November."

Pause.

"I think," says Mr. Boke, "that Chilla is with child."

Quick smile, little bow of pleased acknowledgment. Then, in a narrative voice: "*Je vais dire ça en français. Nous venions d'arriver—*"

"Show them the President's letter," says Mrs. Coover.

"We had just got there," Lance continues, "and Denny was still alive, and the first thing he and I saw—"

In a sudden flutter, Nurse Coover interrupts: "No, Lance, no. No, Madam, please. No contacts, doctor's orders, *please.*"

Warm temple, cold ear.

Mr. and Mrs. Boke are ushered out. They walk swiftly—although there is no hurry, no hurry whatever, down the corridor, along its shoddy, olive-and-ocher wall, the lower olive separated from the upper ocher by a continuous brown line leading to the venerable elevators. Going up (glimpse of patriarch in wheel-chair). Going back in November (Lancelin). Going down (the old Bokes). There are, in that elevator, two smiling women and, the object of their bright sympathy, a girl with a baby, besides the gray-haired, bent, sullen elevator man, who stands with his back to everybody.

Ithaca, 1952.

THE AURELIAN; CLOUD, CASTLE, LAKE; and SPRING IN FIALTA were originally written in Russian. They were first published (as *"Pilgram," "Oblako, ozero, bashnya,"* and *"Vesna v Fial'te"*) in the Russian émigré review *"Sovremennïe Zapiski"* (Paris, 1931, 1937, 1938) under my pen name "V. Sirin" and were incorporated in my collections of short stories (*"Soglyadatay," Russkie Zapiski* publisher, Paris, 1938, and *"Vesna v Fial'te i drugie rasskazi,"* The Chekhov Publishing House, New York, 1956). The English versions of those three stories were prepared by me (who am alone responsible for any discrepancies between them and the original texts) in collaboration with Peter Pertzov. THE AURELIAN and CLOUD, CASTLE, LAKE came out in the *Atlantic Monthly*, and SPRING IN FIALTA in *Harper's Bazaar*, and all three appeared among the NINE STORIES brought out by New Directions in "Direction," 1947.

MADEMOISELLE O was originally written in French and was first published in the review *"Mesures,"* Paris, 1939. It was translated into English with the kind assistance of the late Miss Hilda Ward, and came out in the *Atlantic Monthly* and in the NINE STORIES. A final, slightly different version, with stricter adherence to autobiographical truth, appeared as "Chapter Five" in my memoir CONCLUSIVE EVIDENCE, Harper & Brothers, New York, 1951 (also published in England as SPEAK, MEMORY, by Victor Gollancz, 1952).

The remaining stories in the present volume were written in English. Of these A FORGOTTEN POET, THE ASSISTANT PRODUCER, THAT IN ALEPPO ONCE and TIME AND EBB appeared in the *Atlantic Monthly* and in NINE STORIES; CONVERSATION PIECE (as "Double Talk"), SIGNS AND SYMBOLS, FIRST LOVE (as "Colette"), and LANCE came out first in *The New Yorker;* "Double Talk" was reprinted in NINE STORIES; "Colette", in *The New Yorker* anthology and (as "Chapter Seven") in CONCLUSIVE EVIDENCE; and SCENES FROM THE LIFE OF A DOUBLE MONSTER appeared in *The Reporter*.

Only MADEMOISELLE O and FIRST LOVE are (except for a change of names) true in every detail to the author's remembered life. THE ASSISTANT PRODUCER is based on actual facts. As to the rest, I am no more guilty of imitating "real life" than "real life" is responsible for plagiarizing me.